RED HOT

CAT JOHNSON

New York Times & USA Today Bestselling Author

Kissing Books
Red Hot
Honey Buns

CHAPTER ONE

Red

Something felt . . . off.

The moment I stepped through the back door of the store, almost but not quite late, I sensed it.

Juggling my *Red's Resale* logo coffee mug in one hand, and my keys in the other, I closed the door behind me and moved farther inside.

I did a visual sweep of the work area in the back of the consignment shop, searching for the source of my discomfort.

It wasn't an easy task with my eyes still slits because I had yet to actually consume the level of caffeine I required to make it through another day of retail. Although some days I felt like I needed something a little stronger than coffee to deal with the fine folks of Mudville and its surrounding towns.

In the back office, I checked the handle on the door of the safe where I kept the cash drawer.

Still locked.

I set down both the keys and the coffee on my desk and moved out to the retail area.

Things were everywhere—but that was usual for

my store. For all resale shops actually. At least the busy ones.

I'd been slammed yesterday, so I hadn't had a chance to straighten up the sales floor before closing. And I'd been too tired and hungry to stay late just to clean. I figured I could do it this morning before it got hectic for the day.

Still, something seemed wrong.

Odd. I'd been the last one here last night. I'd locked up, myself, alone. No one should have been here since.

I had to be imagining things.

With no evidence to support the nagging feeling, I moved to the front, turned the *Closed* sign to *Open*, and flipped the deadbolt to unlock the door.

Grabbing my mug again, I carried my much-needed coffee to the front and started to put the store back together into some semblance of neatness. An impossible task given the inconceivable mix of one-of-a-kind items I had to work with, but I attempted it, none-the-less.

In fact, I'd had a great new idea for a display wake me up in the middle of the night. I was going to make one whole area all red since Valentine's Day was just a few weeks away.

The new red-soled Louboutin black heels that I'd just gotten in for consignment yesterday would make the perfect centerpiece, along with the red Birkin bag that came in last week. And I'd just gotten in a gorgeous red buffalo plaid wool cape that would complete the outfit to perfection.

Excited, I ran to the back where I'd managed to get the cape onto a hanger last night but hadn't had time to tag it yet.

I stopped in front of the rack, frowning. The cape should have been hanging right in front.

It wasn't.

Sliding the hangers on the rod, I checked the rest of the clothes, looking for a flash of red and finding none. I bent at the waist and checked the floor below the rack, thinking it might have fallen off the hanger.

Nothing.

Sighing, I straightened. Was I going crazy? Had I moved the cape somewhere and forgot?

I was overworked, not to mention scattered and forgetful at times, but I'd lived like that since the day I'd decided to open Red's Resale. That's when the craziness that was my current life began. I was used to it after all these years.

Maybe Gretchen had come in last night? The girl who sometimes opened and closed the shop for me so I could pretend I had some semblance of a life had a key to the back door.

Pulling my cell out of my pocket, I hit the contact listing for Gretchen.

I waited through the ringing, taking a quick glance at the time on the vintage Mickey Mouse watch on my wrist.

It wasn't too early to call her on her morning off. Since I'd been running a little late myself and slid in right at the shop's scheduled time to open, the hour was late enough I didn't have to feel at all bad.

"Hello."

"Gretchen. Hey, girl. How are you?"

"Good. Really good, actually."

"What's going on?" I asked, intrigued enough to sideline the question about the missing cape for a minute. "I hear a smile in your voice."

"Oh, my God, Red. It's so amazing. You won't believe it."

I stayed quiet and let her talk. Knowing the pause in the words was because she was sucking in a breath, not because she was actually done speaking.

"He asked me," Gretchen squealed.

My eyes widened. "To the dance?"

"Yes!"

For a moment I got to forget I had a heating oil bill sitting on my desk that needed paying, and that I had to do payroll today. I could pretend I didn't have to be a responsible adult and instead could channel Gretchen's high school senior enthusiasm at having the boy she liked ask her to the dance.

"That's amazing. I'm so happy for you."

"I'm hoping that pink dress I liked is still on the rack upstairs." Gretchen's comment brought me immediately back to the reason I'd called. The store. Namely, the missing stock.

"Um, Gretchen, any chance you stopped in the shop last night and moved the red and black buffalo plaid cape that was hanging in the back waiting to be

4

tagged?"

"What? No. I went right home from practice to eat and shower. Then he called and asked me, and I spent the rest of the night on video chat with my friends."

That sounded about right. It wasn't that many years ago I was her age. Okay, more than a decade, but still, I could remember.

"Okay. Thanks. And I'll run upstairs right now and pull that dress off sale and put it in back for you."

"Thank you! I'll be in this afternoon to work."

"Yup. See you then. Bye."

She said goodbye and I disconnected the call, still as baffled as I'd been before.

Grabbing my coffee mug, I cradled it and glanced around me. Things didn't walk away on their own.

Okay, I had found those couple of mouse turds in the back office last year, but that was my own fault for leaving food out. That situation had been remedied and since then I'd seen no evidence of the scurrying rodent variety.

Besides, that would have to be one heck of a huge mouse to carry away a wool cape.

We'd all have bigger problems than a missing piece of merchandise if the rodents of Mudville grew apocalyptically big . . . although I have wondered on occasion what horrors had been dumped into the Muddy River over the centuries.

Pushing my science fiction fantasies aside, I decided to walk through the entire shop and see if anything else looked out of place. Or more out of place than usual, I amended as I almost tripped over a tricycle that I needed to carry downstairs to the toy area.

The basement level of the store was as good a place as any to start. I downed the remainder of the coffee and moved in back to set the cup in the sink . . . and noticed it was wet. Water drops beaded on the porcelain bowl. I ran my fingers over the drops, to make sure it wasn't an optical illusion, and rubbed my thumb over my wet forefinger.

Even if I had run the water last night right before I'd closed at six, water wouldn't remain in the sink for sixteen hours with the heat running in the shop. It would have been dry by now.

Maybe the faucett was dripping. It might need tightening or a new gasket or something. I'd have to keep an eye on it and fix it right away if it was leaking. My water bill was already high enough.

Adding one more thing on my mental To Do list, I spun back to the front, grabbed the tricycle by the handlebar and headed downstairs, flipping on the wall switches for the lights as I walked past them.

I set the bike down and stared at the corner display. Something looked different there too, though I couldn't quite put my finger on it.

The basement housed sporting goods, children's toys, pet supplies and men's clothing. I didn't spend a whole lot of time down here, but I remembered the table being fuller than it was now.

Letting out a sigh, I shook my head. I was losing my mind—or I had a thief.

A thief who didn't touch the fine jewelry display but had grabbed something from the basement and a ladies' cape? That seemed odd. But this was Mudville. Odd was our middle name.

I smiled and considered having some T-shirts printed up. *Welcome to Mudville, New York. Odd is our middle name.*

I'd have to work on that wording a bit.

Maybe Harper could help me with a good slogan. She was the local writer. She should be able to figure out something great.

Happy with that plan, I climbed the stairs, all the way up to the second floor. I immediately spotted the pink dress Gretchen wanted. At least that was where it was supposed to be.

Maybe I wasn't ready for the looney bin quite yet. But something was definitely up and I was going to get to the bottom of it. Hopefully.

Holding the pink dress out in front of me, I remembered seeing a vintage clutch that would go perfectly with it. It was downstairs in the purse room . . . or at least I hoped it was still there.

I held the dress up and saw what might be a stain on the bodice as it caught the sunlight streaming in the window. I hadn't noticed it before.

Crud. I really needed to get that electrician to come back and install better lighting downstairs where I took in the consignments so I could see what I was really getting. And I'd have to get this dry cleaned for Gretchen. I didn't want her wearing a stained dress to the dance and telling everyone it came from here.

Spinning, while still eying the possible stain, I took one step and smashed into something or someone blocking my way.

And, of course, I screamed. Not that there'd be anyone to hear me in this big old Victorian turned storefront.

"Red! It's us."

I lowered the dress, which I'd been holding up in front of me like a shield. Because tulle made such good protection. I resisted the urge to roll my eyes at myself and tried to recover from the fright when I saw my two girlfriends standing there.

Harper cringed. "Sorry we scared you."

"She'll recover." Bethany held out a paper bag. "I brought honey buns, fresh and hot, right out of the oven."

"In that case, I forgive you." I snatched the offering from the town baker.

Opening the bag, I stuck my nose inside, inhaling the amazing aroma that hit me in a sweet cloud of steamy air. "Come on downstairs so we can talk and I can watch the front door at the same time."

Actually, I wanted to talk and eat, while I watched for customers. No hot honey bun was going to get cold on my watch. And I could brew another cup of coffee while I was there, to go along with my confections.

But fresh baked goods and more caffeine aside, that my two friends had snuck up on me proved I really was in a complete bubble on the second floor. Anything at all could be happening downstairs and I wouldn't know.

That's probably why things were going missing.

This whole place really needed a good security system. More than just those couple of cameras I'd bought and never actually gotten around to hooking up. Something else for the To Do list.

We reached the first floor and, thankfully, it looked like nothing had changed since I'd gone upstairs. I led the way to the coffee maker and popped in a pod.

"What has you two out and about so early?" I asked.

Bethany frowned. "Ten isn't early. I was at the bakery at six."

"Fine," I conceded. "But I don't keep baker's hours. And neither does Harper."

"Actually, I was up writing at five. But I got my wordcount done for the day and decided to celebrate by walking down to get a treat at Bethany's. And since she could sneak away for a minute while her assistant is there, we decided to come see you."

My friends were obviously crazy. Not for wanting to visit with me—I was an absolute delight so of course they'd want to visit. But to be at work before sunrise? Pfft. Forget about that lunacy.

Apparently, I was the only one among us who actually liked to sleep. Having the shop open at ten daily was early enough for me.

This was clearly a no-win debate, so I moved on. "So, weird stuff is happening."

"Weird how?" Harper drew back, her dark brows drawn low over her eyes.

"Why do you look so scared?" Bethany asked Harper.

"Because it could be her ghost. Is it your ghost?" Harper spun to ask me, looking ready to bolt as her gaze cut to the side where the basement door was located.

I let out a snort. "Unless the ghost has a penchant for buffalo plaid wool capes, I think I'm good."

Harper's mouth formed a perfect O to match her widened eyes. "Ooo. That sounds cute. Red and black?"

"Yup. And it would look so good on you with black leggings and boots." I nodded.

"It sounds adorable. But what does this cape have to do with ghosts?" Bethany asked.

"It doesn't. I hope. But the cape is missing. I put it right there on the rack last night and it's gone this morning. And other stuff feels . . . off. I called Gretchen. She wasn't here."

"It seems odd for someone to break in and only take one thing," Bethany commented.

"Exactly." I nodded. "That's what I thought. Especially since there are far more valuable things around here to take."

"You sure you didn't stash it away somewhere and forget?" Bethany suggested. "You have been known to forget things."

"Nope." I shook my head, refusing to admit she was right and I had, in past, forgotten a thing or two. "I know because it came in right before closing and I still had to tag it and enter it into inventory. I was going to do that first thing this morning."

Harper shook her head, lips compressed into an unhappy line. "I think you need to go over and report it to that hot deputy at the sheriff's department."

"Hot deputy?" I shot Harper a meaningful glance, knowing without asking she meant Carson Bekker, who was the only one at the sheriff's department who would fit that description. I lifted a brow. "Does your boyfriend know you think Carson is hot?"

Harper waved off my concern. "Stone knows it's purely a professional interest I have in the deputy."

Bethany let out a burst of a laugh. "Professional interest? How's that?"

"I'm writing a hero who's a deputy. Carson is my inspiration. That's all." Harper lifted one shoulder innocently.

I shook my head. "You get away with a lot by using that 'I'm a writer' excuse."

Harper smiled. "I really do. But it's the truth. Besides, I'm head over heels for Stone. You know that. He knows that. Mary Brimley, the town gossip, knows that."

"Aunt Agnes, who told you to build a soundproof sex room in the attic so she won't have to hear you two going at it, knows that." I smirked.

Harper cringed. "Don't remind me. Talking about that stuff with my septuagenarian great aunt is not high on my list of things to do."

Bethany leaned close to me. "There she goes using those big words again."

"I know. Right? I installed a dictionary app on my phone because of her." I eyed Harper with a cocked brow.

Harper rolled her eyes. "Anyway, I'm serious. You should at least have an official report filed and on record. That way if you do catch the person, or more stuff is missing, there's a paper trail and you have some legal recourse."

"I know. I should." I knew Harper was right, even if I didn't like it. I sighed and glanced at Bethany. "You have any more of these honey buns at the shop?"

"I sure do. Can't run out of my signature item."

"I'll take a box full." I figured if I was going to send the sheriff's department on a wild goose chase for a misplaced cape, which might or might not have been stolen, I should at least sweeten the deal.

CHAPTER TWO

Cash

"Cashel."

I stopped with the steaming mug halfway to my mouth. "Yes, Mother."

She paused on her way through the kitchen with a basket of laundry in her hands. "I need more firewood brought in, when you get a chance."

The first thing I did was glance around to see if I could spot one of my two brothers.

Passing the buck was a long-standing tradition in this family. If I could get Boone or Stone to do something instead of me, damn right I was going to.

Not seeing anyone, the next best thing I could do was get creative with my reply. "I'll see it gets done today."

I didn't say I would do it. Just that it would get done.

Happy with my genius, I returned my mother's smile and proceeded to take the first sip of piping hot coffee. The scorching liquid felt good sliding down my throat, warming me from the inside.

It was freaking cold out there. Just because the farm stand was closed until spring didn't mean work stopped. Owning and operating Morgan Farm was a year-round endeavor. There were no days off on a farm. No *snow days* for that matter either.

After being outside at the crack of dawn, feeding and watering the animals, I needed this cup of liquid heat.

I fully intended to warm up before I even thought about going outside again, for any reason. And I figured the longer I procrastinated getting that firewood, the more chance Boone or Stone would wander through and I could get them to do it. Or at least get them to help with the work that had landed on me just because I'd had the misfortune of standing here while our mother walked by.

It would be the perfect plan, except that Stone spent more time at his girlfriend's place than home lately. My older brother was getting harder and harder to pass tasks off to.

And my younger brother—well, he was just Boone being Boone. Young. Flighty. Eager and willing, but hard to pin down. Boone was like a hound who'd seen a squirrel. He rushed from one thing to the next, be that an odd job for the people in town or the next woman in his life.

It was pretty obvious to me that middle siblings were the smartest. Not to mention the most even-tempered, clever and, no doubt, handsome.

I wasn't tied down to one woman, at her beck and call—and at her aunt's too—twenty-four seven like Stone was with Harper. Nor was I running off trying to juggle a multitude of women—and hobbies and odd jobs—like Boone.

Nope. Mine was a simple life. Just the way I liked it. Working on my family's farm. Hanging out at the local bar. Swinging by town to see what was what. Maybe popping in to visit one pretty little shop keeper on Main Street.

"Cash!"

"What?" I called back in response to my father, who'd bellowed to me from another room.

"These boxes full of Christmas decorations still have to get put upstairs."

Shit. Now I had two things to pass off to my brothers and if I stuck around much longer, I had no doubt that number would grow.

Tasty hot coffee aside, hanging out in this location clearly wasn't working for me. Time to go.

"I'll see it gets done," I promised, once again using my favorite new reply. "I'm heading out now. Be back later," I called to whoever was still in hearing distance.

I downed my final sip of coffee, set my mug in the dishwasher and skedaddled, anxious to get out the door before my lengthening list of potential chores got any longer.

Glancing at the time displayed on the dashboard in the truck, I realized it was too early to hit the bar. So, to town it was.

Maybe Bethany would have something good coming out of the oven. I could grab an extra pastry and swing by Red's with it . . . just to say howdy.

I liked to be neighborly. It would be a courtesy, from one Mudville small business owner to another.

I was all about good relations. Especially when they were with the red headed owner of Mudville's premiere resale shop.

I'd hit the bakery and then head directly to Red's. I knew I had to get there before lunch or her helper came in to work and then sometimes Red wouldn't be there.

Not that I'd memorized her schedule or anything. Or that I went to the shop *only* to see Red. Of course not. I bought stuff there too. Some good shit came into the store.

At least it was *good shit* to a person who had an appreciation for odd gadgets and pre-worn clothes. Apparently, I happened to be one of those people. I owned more stuff than any man should and that was mostly because of my frequent stops at Red's.

My idea to swing by Bethany's for something sweet, then backtrack to Red's with it, was derailed by the sight of a sheriff's department vehicle parked in Red's lot.

Something must be wrong.

That realization put the brakes on my plan—literally.

I slammed my foot on the brake pedal and careened off Main Street, swinging the truck down the side street too fast.

My pickup skidded to a rough stop in the gravel of the resale shop's parking lot. I didn't even take the time to pull the key out of the ignition after I cut the engine as I jumped out of the truck and sprinted toward the steps.

Breathless, I flung the door wide and leapt over the threshold. A warm burst of air from inside hit me at the same time as Red's tinkling laugh.

Her girlish giggle was answered by a deep, throaty and definitely masculine chuckle.

Eyes narrowed, teeth clenched, I shoved the door closed behind me, hard enough it sounded like the little bell might come flying off. I'd been worried to death about her, and here she was laughing?

Not just laughing, but flirting with the good deputy himself, by the looks of things.

I strode across the store, past displays of random dust catchers, directly to the cash register.

There was Red, leaning her elbows on the counter next to a platter overflowing with sticky buns. The same sticky buns I'd been planning to pick up for her, before I was waylaid by panic over her well-being.

But it was the guy who had his ass perched on the edge of that counter who really grabbed my attention . . . and pissed me off. He was biting into one of the honey buns while looking at Red like he wanted to take a bite out of her.

"Cash. Hi," Red greeted me, as sweetly as ever.

Then again, retail was her livelihood. She had to be sweet to everybody. It was good business.

"Red." My gaze moved from her to land on the man in the deputy's uniform. "Carson."

"Cash." He met my stare head on, then moved on to grinning at Red again. "But really. You didn't have to bribe me with pastries just to get me over here."

Did that fucker's eyes just drop to look down Red's T-shirt before he yanked his gaze back up?

Son of a bitch. I felt my jaw clench.

"Eh, I thought it couldn't hurt." She shrugged, still smiling too brightly at him.

What was going on here? This didn't look like an official visit. And if it wasn't official business, why were Red and Carson all cozied up?

I tipped my chin to the plate of pastries. "Trying something new? Is it customer appreciation hour or something?" I asked, trying to get to the bottom of the situation without it being obvious that's what I was doing.

Frowning, she followed my gaze and glanced down at the plate, before her eyes widened. "Oh, you mean the honey buns. No, I just thought I should get something for Carson since he drove all the way over here after I called him."

Red and I had both graduated high school with Carson a decade ago. I'd liked the guy back then when we'd both played football for Mudville High.

Hell, I'd liked him right up until just now, when I'd found him moving in on Red.

Now, I wanted to tackle the former quarterback and deliver some pain like I used to during practice.

"And I told her, it's my job to check things out when someone calls the department with a report," Carson continued.

So, this *was* official business in spite of all appearances to the contrary.

Why didn't that make me feel better? I felt my brows creep up at his casual attitude, and how damn close he was sitting and leaning in toward where Red stood.

"I have to agree with him, Red. It is his job. And bribery of an officer of the law is a crime," I said.

She leveled a confused stare on me. "Bethany's honey buns are the best, but I'm not sure they'd count as bribery."

Carson leaned in closer to her. "Don't worry, Freckles. I won't turn you in." He grinned and winked at her before popping the last bite into his mouth and licking his fingers.

Freckles. I'd forgotten Carson used to tease Red and call her that back in school.

Except now, unlike then, the nickname didn't sound like schoolboy teasing anymore. It— accompanied by his sly smirk and wink—seemed decidedly flirty. Almost wolfish, like Carson was on the prowl and Red was the nearest lamb he wanted to sink his flashing white teeth into.

Mother fucker. I wasn't imagining it. He was hitting on Red.

Eyes narrowed, I swung my gaze from him to her and didn't like what I saw. Red's cheeks had gotten all flushed at his teasing.

Time to change the subject.

"So, why'd you have to call the sheriff's department? What happened? Everything all right?" I asked.

I could only hope she had actually called the department phone and Carson had been on duty at the time to answer the call. Otherwise, that meant she'd called his cell directly. I couldn't even wrap my head around the idea of Red and Carson calling or texting each other.

That would be too frigging cozy.

Hell, even I didn't text Red. And I could if I wanted to. I had her number. I just preferred dropping by. Though, by the looks of this little scene I'd stumbled upon, so did Carson.

"It's nothing. Really." Red waved off my question.

I frowned. "It had to have been something or you wouldn't have called him." I tipped my head toward Carson.

"It's just . . . it's silly really, but something went missing overnight. And some other things just felt odd. Out of place. It's probably nothing."

I wasn't as willing to dismiss it as easily as Red had. I spotted the camera in the corner. "Don't you have security footage you can look at?"

Her face turned a deep red. "No. Those, uh, don't actually work."

"What?" My eyes widened.

Carson chuckled. "I've already been through all this with her, Cash. Don't bother."

20

I didn't listen to him and forged ahead. "Why don't they work?"

She planted a hand on each hip. "Because I'm a little busy around here and never got around to actually hooking them up."

"Jesus, Red." I looked to the ceiling for patience. "You do have a working alarm at least, right?"

"Um . . ." Her lack of an answer had me letting out a blue streak of language not appropriate for a lady to hear. But I figured Red deserved to hear it, given her lack of concern for her own safety.

I pulled off my jacket. "I'm taking care of this right now."

Her eyes widened. "What? What do you mean?"

"I'm at least getting the cameras hooked up. Then we're going to discuss the alarm situation."

"And on that note, I'll be leaving." Carson pushed off the counter and stood to his full height. And, dammit, how I hated he was a good two inches taller than my own six feet. He continued, "I'll give you a call once I type everything up and have an official copy of the report for you, to make sure you're here before I stop by and drop it off."

Oh, great. Another visit. I rolled my eyes at his excuse to stop in and see her again.

"I don't want you to have to come all the way over here with it. I can come pick it up—"

"Here's an idea," Carson began. "How about we meet halfway. The Muddy River Inn sound good? When I have the report ready, I'll give you a call and we can meet at Lainey's. It's been too long since I've had her hot wings. And I bet they'd taste even better if I share them with you."

The bastard! There had to be some sort of law about a deputy conducting official sheriff's business at a bar. If there was, I planned on finding it.

"Um, all right. Yeah. Sure. Thank you. And please, take these with you." She lifted the platter of honey buns toward him, without even offering me one, I noticed.

Carson shook his head. "Nope. Better keep those here. The sheriff is on a strict diet. His wife's orders. He'll get real cranky if he even sees these."

"All right." She put down the platter and walked around the counter to follow Carson to the door, as if the man couldn't find his own way the couple of yards there. "Thank you so much for coming over."

"Any time. I mean that. I'll be calling you soon about those hot wings."

Red nodded. "Okay."

Carson shot Red one more lascivious glance and then the bastard had the nerve to wink at her again. What the fuck was that about? This was certainly not professional behavior.

As my blood pressure rose, he lifted his gaze to me. "Later, Cash."

"Yup," I shot back.

Much, much later, hopefully.

As angry as I was hungry, I grabbed one of Carson's leftover honey buns and tore off a bite.

I was still chewing when Red finally closed the door behind him and turned back toward me.

"I'm eating one of these," I said with my mouth full.

"That's fine. You're welcome to them," she said.

Humph. A leftover pastry wasn't a date for drinks and wings at the bar like Carson had gotten, but at least it was something.

"So, what went missing?" I asked after swallowing the sticky, sweet confection and wishing I had a cup of coffee to go with it.

"It was just a cape." She shrugged. "Bethany's probably right. I probably misplaced it. It'll turn up, and when it does, I can feel stupid and apologize to Carson for bothering him."

I didn't know why she was acting like this missing item didn't matter. It obviously did. Enough she'd called the sheriff about it. And I really didn't want her calling Carson to apologize. Or worse, to try and make it up to him somehow with more than just hot wings.

Putting the uneaten half of the honey bun on a napkin, I shook my head. "Don't you worry about bothering Carson. He and John Callahan got nothing else to do over there at the sheriff's department. At least not anymore now that folks stopped breaking into Agnes's house to steal those damn diaries out of the attic."

Red snorted out a laugh. "That's true. Stealing them wouldn't do any good now anyway. Not since Harper scanned every page of them. All eighty-five years' worth of Rose's journals are digital and safely stored in the cloud, according to her."

"Harper did all that?"

Jeez. Apparently, my brother wasn't keeping his girl busy enough if she had time to do that kind of shit.

Red nodded. "Yup. She's a little obsessive like that."

I had to agree and hopped down off the counter where I'd taken over Carson's spot. I'd figured if Carson could sit on Red's counter, I sure as fuck could too.

"Let's see that camera set up."

"You're looking at it." Her cheeks reddened again.

"What do you mean?"

"I mean I took the cameras out of the box, stuck them up in a couple of places, but never did anything else with them."

Jesus Christ. This woman was exasperating. I sighed. "Are they digital or wired?"

"WiFi. I can monitor them on the computer in the back . . . if they were hooked up."

"Battery or electric?" I needed to figure out if I'd be playing electrician here or just tech support.

"Battery."

"All right. Any chance you have the boxes, or at least the instruction manual?" I asked.

"That I do have. Both."

Miracles never ceased. "Good. Show me."

She trotted toward the back room and I followed at a more leisurely pace.

I might have been engrossed in watching how her hips swayed in those jeans. But I got a hold of myself just in time and remembered to lift my foot for the small step up into the back room rather than trip. Win!

The back room was a minefield of stuff. There was barely enough room for me to plant one foot in front of another.

I had to wonder how Red would even know if something was missing. Bethany was probably right. Chances were that cape was here, just hidden by the avalanche of other stuff.

"Business good?" I asked, glancing around at the over-abundance of merchandise.

"I hear that judgement in your voice, Cashel Morgan. And I'll have you know I would have had most of this tagged and out on the racks for sale already if I didn't spend the morning filing reports with the sheriff's department. And I do have customers to deal with too, you know."

"I know. Did I say anything?" I asked defensively.

My brothers might wrongly accuse me of being an idiot at times, but I knew one thing, and that was not to cross Red Meyer.

"You didn't have to say anything to look judgmental." She scowled.

"Nope. Not me. The more stuff the better, I always say."

"Oh, is that what you always say?" She planted one hand on her hip, attitude dripping from her tone.

"Yup." I nodded. "The more to sell to lucky shoppers, right?"

She eyed me as if deciding whether to believe me or not.

I chose to not give her the chance to fall on the wrong side in her decision making and continued, "So, those instructions for the cameras?"

"Oh, yeah."

I smiled as she was easily deflected from our little tiff and moved on to pawing through the mess on the desk. Her search extended to what was under the desk as I leaned against the wall and enjoyed watching her.

Finally, she emerged with a box. "Got 'em."

She handed it to me just as the high school girl who worked for her on occasion walked through the door. "Hey. I'm here. Where should I start?"

And there went my alone time with Red. But at least today had accomplished one thing.

Two things actually.

First, after I'd straightened out her security in the shop, she'd owe me one. And second, I now knew to keep an eye on my old teammate Carson when it came to Red.

That might be the most important accomplishment of all.

No one was moving in on Red. Not while I was around.

CHAPTER THREE

Red

Cash clicked a few keys on the computer in the back office and suddenly a window for each of the three floors of Red's Resale popped onto the screen. "You can get an overall view of all the cameras at once, or you can zoom in on just one."

"Wow."

I knew he was cute. I also knew he was cocky and full of himself. What I had not known was that Cash was secretly a computer whiz. At least, far better at this kind of stuff than I was.

"It will record and store twenty-four hours of video with the free service. But if you want more than that, they have an annual paid service that gives you thirty-days of cloud storage," he continued his tutorial.

I shook my head. "Who knew?"

Cash cocked one light brown brow high above his hazel eyes. "I would think you would have. You bought them."

"They were on special online last Black Friday. The price was so good I just clicked to buy them." I lifted one shoulder.

"Ah." He looked mildly amused at my impulse purchase.

Happy he'd accepted my explanation and hadn't even criticized it, I moved on. "I don't know how to thank you. This is really amazing."

"It wasn't all that hard. If you'd known your WiFi password I'd have been done an hour ago."

There was the classic Cashel Morgan criticism I'd come to know and love over the years. Or at least know. Love, not so much.

"Hey, I found the sticky note," I defended. *Eventually.*

"You did." He nodded.

I didn't miss how his gaze dropped to take in the drawer I'd pulled apart to look for said sticky note. The contents were now all over the floor of my office.

Subtly I took a step to the side to hide the worst of the mess . . . and stepped on a pen. It sent my foot sliding on the cylindrical obstacle, like wearing roller skates indoors. I toppled forward and landed face down across Cash's lap where he sat in my desk chair.

I dared to glance up and saw the amused expression on his face as he asked, "You okay?"

"Yeah. Sorry."

He shook his head, his gaze taking in my prone position, including my gluteus maximus right there in front of him. "I'm not complaining."

No, he wouldn't.

I knew Cashel Morgan appreciated women. *All* women.

That was the problem. In the ten years since high school he'd never settled down with one, not even for a short while. But that had been true of Stone too, and he was certainly settling in with Harper.

I got my footing and pushed off him, ignoring the heat of his hands on my waist as he helped me stand.

Cash had known me since kindergarten. Back when he put paste and glitter in my hair, so I could be a fairy, he'd said.

If he was interested in me as anything other than a friend, it would have happened before now.

I'd have to be happy that even though he didn't want to date me, at least he wasn't dating anyone else in Mudville.

Clearly the issue was with him. Not me.

So, there you had it. He was just a friend. And he'd done me a big favor today.

"Thank you for doing this," I said. "I really appreciate it."

"You're welcome. But I didn't look at the alarm system yet."

"Oh. That."

He narrowed his eyes. "What does that mean?"

I huffed out a sigh. "The alarm doesn't work because I don't want to spend the money on the monthly service, so I canceled it."

"Red!" He let out a run of cuss words I was glad Gretchen and the customer she was ringing up couldn't hear from the salesfloor.

When he was done, I acknowledged his frustration with me. "I know. But it's expensive."

"Getting robbed is more expensive. No? Not to mention the risk of getting murdered while you're here alone."

I rolled my eyes. "It's Mudville."

"So?"

"So, the old biddies around here see everything. They're better than an alarm system." In fact, maybe I should ask my neighbor if she had seen what happened to the cape.

Harper joked they should get matching *neighborhood watch* T-shirts and she was right.

There was nothing the town gossips missed. If I didn't remember to close my curtains, the old ladies knew everything that was happening inside my apartment. But the joke was on them because usually there was a whole lot of nothing happening at my place.

Certainly nothing of the romantic variety.

"Red, you need to take your security seriously," Cash continued to lecture me.

The shocker was that Cash was taking anything seriously. He was the joker of the family. He'd been voted Class Clown in the Mudville High Senior Class Polls. But he wasn't joking now.

Our gazes met. I'd been about to make a joke myself but being faced with a serious Cash knocked the desire right out of me. At least the desire to make a joke. The other kind of desire was still there. Growing in fact.

I'd crushed on him since I used to sit in the stands through all sorts of weather just to watch him play. My high school football obsession had less to do with my school spirit and more to do with my lusting over Cash.

I'd always been into the young immature joker. But this new mature serious version—that ramped up my interest to a whole other level.

And apparently my renewed and amplified schoolgirl crush stole my ability to defend myself. I had no excuse for my actions, so I had to change the subject.

"Um, so I want to pay you for doing this. Connecting the cameras."

His frown was deep and almost angry. "Fuck that. You're not paying me."

Darn it. Now I'd insulted him somehow. "Um, okay. Sorry."

His gaze hit on the coffee maker. "That thing work?"

"The coffee maker? Yeah. I even have sugar and creamer and everything."

Cash nodded. "Brew me a cup, give me another one of those honey buns and we'll call it even."

That didn't sound even to me, but I knew better

than to fight with a man that stubborn and hardheaded—literally. He'd taken a direct hit to the head in high school during a game that would have leveled any human. But Cash had hopped right back up and finished the quarter.

"Okay," I agreed and moved to grab a clean mug.

As I filled it with water for the single serve coffee maker, I considered that my owing Cash Morgan a favor wasn't such a bad thing.

There were all sorts of tantalizing ways I imagined he could collect on the debt. The question was, after all these years, would he?

As he continued to concentrate on the computer screen instead of me, even as I leaned over him and practically stuck my boobs in his face as I grabbed a coffee pod, I was afraid I had my answer.

CHAPTER FOUR

Cash

The Muddy River Inn was hopping. Nearly every table was full and the lone waitress was running to take care of them all.

The bartender had his hands full too, keeping up with the drink orders from the tables as well as the nearly full bar. The only empty stool was the one next to me.

"Well, well, well. Imagine finding you here." Boone's voice from behind me had me turning on the bar stool.

"Where the hell else would I be?" I said, loud enough he'd be able to hear me over the music blaring from the jukebox.

"True that. Ain't nowhere else to go around here." My younger brother pulled off his jacket and hung it on the back of the empty barstool before settling his ass in for what would, no doubt, be a long visit.

What he'd said was right. There was nowhere else to go around here. And with freezing rain falling now, and the prediction it was turning into snow before too long, going anywhere far was out of the question.

I sure as hell wasn't going to hang around at home. I'd already had to carry in firewood and put the Christmas boxes away, thanks to Stone being conveniently occupied with Harper at her Aunt Agnes's house and Boone taking on another side job. I wasn't going to sit there waiting for more chores to come my way.

Besides, the sadist in me wanted to be here in case Red walked in with that bastard Carson. Hot wings, my sweet ass. That man had more on his mind when it came to Red than chicken.

"Hey." Boone backhanded me in the side and knocked me out of my own head.

"What?" I asked, annoyed.

"I'd asked if you were ready for another one but forget about it now. Buy your own damn beer." He scowled.

"Sorry. I didn't hear you."

"Obviously and I don't think it's because Carter is cranking the music. What's up with you?" Boone asked, frowning as he pinned me with his stare.

"Nothing." I wasn't going to open this topic of discussion with my little brother.

Besides, there was really nothing to say. She could have wings with whoever she wanted. It wasn't like I'd asked her to have wings with me.

Not that I wouldn't enjoy having wings with her—I'm sure we'd both have a good time—but having

34

wings with Red would complicate things.

As Boone stared at me like I had dick antlers, I realized somewhere during the debate happening in my head, *wings* had become equated with sex in my brain.

"Whatever." Boone rolled his eyes at me then glanced to see where Carter was. "Hey, I'm kinda hungry. You wanna share an order of wings with me?"

I nearly choked on the swallow of beer I'd had the misfortune of taking when he'd asked the incredibly poorly timed question.

After I finally recovered from my coughing fit, I wiped away the moisture from my eyes that almost choking to death had caused and shook my head.

When I could see again, none other than Carson was standing in the doorway. *Fuck.*

I turned away from the door and realized Boone was still waiting for an answer. "No. I don't want wings."

Boone shot me an incredulous glance. Probably because I'd never said no to food before. "Suit yourself. I'll eat them all on my own then."

I didn't have an appetite any longer because I had a bad feeling Carson wasn't going to be alone for long, especially when I saw him make his way to a little table for two in the back.

Yup, that would be the table I'd choose if I was meeting Red tonight. Nestled in the corner away from the crowd and the noise.

As I scowled, shooting him daggers he didn't even see, Carson stood and, eyes pinned on the door behind me, lifted one arm, waving someone over.

I didn't need to turn to see who it was. I did anyway, twisting in my seat after a bracing swallow of beer.

There she was, standing just inside the doorway stomping the snow off her boots on the mat. Her cheeks were pink from the cold outside. Her blue eyes bright as she looked around her.

My only solace was that she saw me first, before she spotted Carson. That wasn't hard since the door was right by the bar.

She gave me a tightlipped smile and a small wave before her gaze cut to the seating area. It didn't take her long to spot Carson with as tall as he was. Not to mention that, in addition to his arm flailing to get Red's attention, he was now striding forward.

I watched her smile. Watched him press one hand against her back and lead her toward the table. I even turned so I could follow their progress all the way to the back where he pulled her chair out for her.

"Ah. Now I get it."

Lips pressed tight, I turned back to face the bar. Elbows braced against the rail I sighed and asked, "Get what?"

"Why you're in such a piss poor mood you don't even want Lainey's hot wings."

Fucking wings. Even the sound of the word grated on my nerves as I remembered Carson's invitation to Red.

I bet they'd taste even better if I share them with you.

Ugh!

The sound of my little brother laughing had me frowning.

I felt the scowl settle in. I had a feeling it wasn't going to go away any time soon. And Boone's laughing at me didn't help.

"Fuck you," I grumbled.

Boone was undeterred. It took more than me cussing at him to affect my little bro. But my outburst had been more to make me feel better than to hurt him. Unfortunately, it failed. I still felt like shit.

"You should have asked her out long ago. She always liked you."

I remained quiet, knowing he was right.

"Now? I don't know. Looks like it might be too late." Boone's gaze cut to the back corner of the room.

I refused to look again, but I couldn't let his misinterpretation of the situation stand.

"No. This is a business meeting," I corrected.

Boone's brows lifted. "What kind of meeting?"

I wasn't about to go spilling Red's business in public so I tried to keep it vague. "He's just giving her a copy of some paperwork."

"Seems to me there are other ways to deliver a piece of paper than meeting at a bar at night."

Inwardly, I agreed. Outwardly, I was getting ornerier by the minute.

"Yeah, well, that's how they decided to do it so just leave it alone." Scowling, I reached for my pint glass, downed the remains and pushed the couple of dollars on the bar in front of me forward for Carter's tip. "I'm gonna go."

"Home?" Boone asked.

"Yeah. No. I don't know. Maybe." I had nowhere else to go on a shit night like this, but I hated to admit that to Boone. I stood and reached for my jacket. "I'll see you later."

"All right." Boone eyed me and I suspected what he was thinking. He'd be in no rush to see me later if I was still in this crappy mood.

I couldn't blame him. I couldn't stand my own company at the moment. I shouldn't expect anyone else to.

My indecision about going home or not ended as I found myself parked down the block on the side street of Red's place. From there I could see the shop and the old carriage house in the back yard that she'd converted into an apartment for herself.

If Carson came home with her, I'd see it.

This wasn't stalker behavior at all. Nope. I sighed and cut the engine and the lights, settling in for the duration. Whether she came home with Carson or if she didn't, I knew I wouldn't be able to rest until I knew which.

I expected a long cold wait.

What I didn't expect was to see the beam of a flashlight skitter across the small yard in the back of the shop. *What the fuck?*

CHAPTER FIVE

Red

Carson was handsome, no doubt. And the deputy sheriff's uniform he wore on the job didn't hurt. Not one bit.

Harper had been right to base a character in her next book on him. He had all the makings of a romance hero.

So why did my stomach drop when I saw Cash walking out the door? And why did I keep checking my phone to see what time it was or if I had any texts instead of paying attention to the man seated next to me?

Because I was a glutton for punishment, apparently.

Did I have a problem? Was I only interested in men who didn't want me? If my obsession with Cash was any indication, I might have issues.

"Oh, I almost forgot." The warmth of Carson's hand landing on top of mine on the table caught my attention.

"Forgot what?" I asked, pulling my hand out from under his and reaching for my glass.

"The report." Looking undeterred that I'd extricated my hand from his, Carson reached into the inside pocket of the jacket he'd hung on the back of the chair.

He drew out a folded piece of paper. "Here you go."

I took it, staring first at it and then up at him. "Thanks. Um, what am I supposed to do with it?"

He laughed. "Nothing. Just keep it with your important papers. Just in case. We have a copy at the department."

So, I really didn't need it at all then. And chances were good I'd misplace it and never be able to find it again if there ever did arise a need. And then I'd have to go to the sheriff's department to get another copy anyway.

I kept all those predictions of what no doubt would be the future of this paper to myself and tried to seem grateful. "Okay. Thanks."

"No problem. My pleasure." He smiled and I was treated to a flash of straight white teeth.

This man was male model handsome. And a model citizen. He'd probably be a model boyfriend too.

The problem was, there was no spark. I liked him well enough—but that was the extent of it.

Could I base a relationship just on friendship alone?

I smothered a laugh at my own silliness. Who said Carson even wanted to start a relationship with me? Maybe this was exactly what he'd said. Just two people sharing some really good hot wings.

"So, did you notice anything else at the shop? Anything missing or moved?" he asked.

I shook my head. "No. But we got really busy right after lunch. I wouldn't have had time to notice anything."

He nodded and pulled out his wallet. He slid a business card out and across the table to me. "If you do, you give me a call. Okay? My personal cell phone number is on there. Day or night, you contact me if you need me."

Great. Something else for me to misplace. I picked up the card and put it on top of the folded report. "Thanks."

"No problem." He smiled and laid his hand over mind again.

And I had my answer. I wasn't being silly. Judging by all the hand holding, it was looking like Carson did want to start something with me.

One more time I slipped my hand from beneath his and reached for my glass. It was like my own private drinking game. If this kept up and I had to drink every time Carson tried to hold my hand, I was going to be trashed before the food arrived.

I blew out a breath and glanced around for the waitress, vainly hoping our order of hot wings with the side of fried pickles was on its way to our table.

Of course, it wasn't. The place was mobbed at

night. The kitchen was probably all backed up with orders.

Sighing, I turned back to Carson. "So, that was some season the Hogs had, huh?"

He smiled, looking excited to talk about the football team at our high school.

The conversation remained at that level of riveting for the remainder of the hour.

We talked about the horse that had escaped from one of the local farms, which still eluded capture, and also the bull that had escaped from the local stock auction. He had been, thankfully, caught after a wild week on the lam.

That all, of course, brought up fond memories of when Agnes's pig Petunia had been on the run from the auction before Agnes caught her and the town officially made her the school's mascot so she'd be allowed to live in town.

When I ran out of small talk, I even threw Harper under the bus. I told Carson she was writing a character who was a small-town deputy, which was loosely based on him.

She'd forgive me and I was desperate. At least I didn't tell him she'd called him hot.

Finally, the wings were gone, the table cleared and the bill paid—whether I liked it or not. Carson had insisted on paying for me.

I'd offered to pay, and then suggested we split the bill when he refused my first offer. But he ended up snatching it and going directly to the bartender with it. It made this feel too much like a date.

I didn't want this to be a date.

We were friends and friends I wanted us to stay. Just friends. No benefits. Well, except for the benefit that he'd come investigate my groundless reports of possibly imaginary theft from the shop without judgement.

But I wasn't sure Carson saw things the same way as I did regarding our non-date. Which begged the question, how was the end of this night going to go?

At least I'd met him here, so there wouldn't be that awkward *goodnight* at my door. Though there might be an awkward *goodnight* in the parking lot.

I was trying to figure a way to avoid it altogether when Carson's phone buzzed.

He frowned down at the display and then glanced up at me. "John's at the department alone and wants me to bring him dinner. He called in the order. I gotta wait for it to be ready and drop it off on my way home."

"That's nice of you. Poor guy, working the night shift. I'm sure he's happy to have a co-worker like you." Seeing the way to a clean escape, I tried not to sound overly excited as I babbled. "So, I'm gonna head out. I've got an early morning tomorrow."

He frowned. "Don't you always open at ten?"

"Yeah, I do. But tomorrow I have to check out an estate sale before I open so . . ." Thankful for that convenient truth, I wrestled my sweater covered arms into my jacket and looped my scarf around my neck. "Thank you so much for dinner and for dropping off the paperwork."

The paper. The whole reason for this non-date tonight. The paper I'd almost forgotten on the table. I grabbed it up now with his card, clutching them in my hand along with my truck keys that I'd fished out of my jacket pocket.

I stood up so fast I knocked my chair over, which worked against my smooth exit. I scrambled to pick it up.

Carson stood too as I righted the chair. "Let me walk you out."

"Oh, don't bother. Really. I'm fine walking myself out. I'm parked right outside the door."

"You bring your truck?" he asked.

"Yeah." I frowned at something I heard in his tone.

He cringed. "You sure you should be driving that thing? Especially in this weather."

That thing?

"Yeah, I'm quite sure. She's good. She hasn't let me down yet." I loved my truck and I wasn't sure how I felt about Carson knocking on her.

"All right." He nodded. "But you have my number if she does."

"Yup. I do." Little did Carson know that now, after that comment, he'd be the last person I called if my truck broke down along the side of the road.

Call me stubborn but I'd walk the two miles in the twenty-six-degree weather rather than admit he was right.

I said one more time, "Thanks again."

44

"You're very welcome. We'll have to do it again some time."

"Yeah. Sure. That'd be nice."

Darn it! Why had I said that?

Because my stupid mother had instilled some very inconvenient manners in me, which included almost never saying no to anything.

I'd deal with that promise later. Now, I had to get out while the getting was good.

"So, have a good night."

"You too." He smiled and grabbed my shoulders, leaning forward as I watched his mouth get closer and closer.

Squinting my eyes, as if that was going to help any, I braced for the inevitable kiss I was helpless to avoid. But it didn't come.

The one thing I hadn't counted on was the fact Carson was a gentleman. He pressed a quick, chaste kiss to my cheek and then dropped his hold on me. "Drive safely."

Phew!

"I will. For sure. Thanks. You too." Ready to slap myself for my continued babbling, I finally cut myself short.

I spun and headed toward the door and ran head-on into Boone Morgan on my way out, slamming into his chest in my quest to reach the exit.

"Woah there. In a hurry?" He grinned, steadying me with both hands on my shoulders.

Of all the people to bowl over in my escape from my non-date with Carson, of course it was Cash's brother I'd run into. Because I had the worst luck in Mudville. No doubt about it.

"Uh, just heading home."

"I think I'll wait to get on the road myself for a few minutes, just in case you drive like you walk." He smiled to show me he was joking.

I rolled my eyes at the hot as heck youngest Morgan brother. All three had been blessed with more good looks than any family had a right to.

Hanging out and joking with Boone was not in my escape plan, but I couldn't go without volleying a reply to his insult, even if it was in jest.

"As if you or your brothers need an excuse to hang out here for hours?" I cocked a brow high in challenge, then said, "Good night, Boone."

He grinned. "G'night, Red."

Finally, I made my way through the gauntlet of patrons and outside. The frigid air felt good on my heated cheeks. At least at first.

The problem with driving a truck from the last century was that it took longer to warm it up than it took to drive the distance home. But this truck was older than I was, by a couple of decades actually. If I wanted her to treat me right, I had to treat her right.

By the time I got my truck warmed up enough to drive, my fingers were painfully cold and I regretted forgetting my gloves at the shop. But luckily the heat was finally blowing out of the vents and it was a short drive home.

46

I'd be in my nice warm apartment in under five minutes and I was more than grateful for that fact as I worked the clutch and shifted my old girl into gear.

I passed Stone's truck, parked on Main Street in front of Agnes's house. Harper was obviously having a good night. I only hoped she remembered she'd promised to be up bright and early tomorrow morning to check out the estate sale with me. I was tempted to text her and interrupt her booty call.

I couldn't really be jealous she was most likely getting lucky since I'd just literally fled from my own date-slash-non-date. I shouldn't be envious, but I kind of was.

She'd found the love of her life. How much longer would it be for me to find mine?

That thought had just crossed my mind when I saw Cash's truck parked on my block.

What the heck?

Fate or karma or something cosmic must have been punishing me for my selfish petty jealousy that one of my best friends was happy and in love. Whatever it was, was now dangling in front of me the one man I wanted, who was also the one man I'd likely never have.

Cosmic lesson or not, it still didn't explain why Cash's truck was here. Unless—

Oh my God! He had better not be dating Pansy Parson. Son of a gun! If Cash started dating my neighbor's daughter, I might have to sell and move.

I was just considering that plan seriously when the door swung open and the man in question stepped out.

Meanwhile I still hadn't turned into my driveway and parked yet. I'd been too paralyzed by the sight of Cash's truck and my wild imaginings. I decided to get out of the street and at least park before the most distracting man on earth got any closer.

By the time I climbed down from the driver's seat, Cash was next to me.

"Hey," he said, his tone flat. Serious.

It was dark, but the security light had flicked on when I'd pulled in so I could see his expression clearly and it was as serious as his tone had been.

"Hey, Cash. What's up?" I asked, starting to get concerned myself. If Cash was serious, something was very wrong.

He'd even been cracking jokes when he'd been carried off the field after an injury freshman year. But here, now, in my driveway he looked like someone had died.

Jeez. Had someone died? My mind shot to Agnes and the fact Stone's truck was parked there.

"Is something wrong?" I asked since he still hadn't answered me.

"Well . . ." he began.

His hesitation ramped up my anxiety. My heart started to pound.

Finally, he continued, "I was, uh, driving by. Before. On my way home from the bar. You know, since it's on my way." He cleared his throat. "Anyway, I saw somebody. It was just a glimpse of a flashlight at first but I decided to check it out. Because you had that stuff go missing."

My eyes widened. "And?"

"There was definitely somebody here but I must have scared him off. I heard somebody running when I got out of the truck. I went after him but it was too late. But when I first saw him, he was by the back door of the shop. I decided to hang out and wait for you. Make sure he didn't come back."

His story was frightening. I wanted to dismiss it as kids up to mischief, cutting through back yards instead of walking around on the road, but I just couldn't.

"Did you call the sheriff?" I asked.

He frowned. "No."

There was a definite attitude in that one word, as if I'd insulted his masculinity or something by suggesting it.

"I mean it's not that I'm not grateful you were here to chase him away. And obviously you handled it on your own, but I just thought it's important to have it on record. You know, along with my report about the missing cape. I can call in the morning—"

"No," he interrupted. "*I'll* call in the morning. I was the one who saw him. I'll make the report."

"Okay." I nodded. "Thanks."

"No problem," he grumbled.

"And thanks again for waiting for me." I said, still trying to smooth his easily ruffled feathers.

But I had more important things to worry about

than Cash's bruised male ego.

I glanced around us at the dark street. It was illuminated only by the far away glow of the streetlights on Main Street. The light didn't really reach down the block on the side street where we stood.

After happily living here alone for the past five years, for the first time ever, I felt uncomfortable.

I didn't want to use the word *afraid*. As an independent single woman, I didn't need a man to be my defender. But I was definitely not looking forward to going upstairs to my apartment alone.

I had the motion light that lit the driveway, but inside the carriage house looked especially dark. I hadn't left any lights on before heading to the bar.

The yawning black windows upstairs where I lived seemed even darker than usual, though I knew that was impossible.

All I needed was to buy a few timers. I could solve this problem tomorrow with one quick trip to the local hardware store.

I could set some lights to go on automatically. That way when I came home after sunset, which was at like four-thirty in the dead of winter, I wasn't walking into a pitch-black apartment.

It was something I should have done long ago. I don't know why I hadn't.

But none of this planning solved anything tonight.

There'd been someone creeping around my shop. My yard. My home. And that had me good and spooked about walking in alone.

Of course, Cash was standing right here. Available. Convenient. I glanced at him now.

I hated with everything in me to ask him for help, twice in one day if I counted this morning, but I didn't see that I had much choice. "Um, would you mind maybe just walking through with me?"

"Actually, I was going to insist on that." After that declaration, he took a step toward my shop as he continued talking. "I think we should walk through the store first and then search the ground floor of the carriage house before your apartment upstairs."

"Um, okay." I had to scramble to keep up with his long legs as he strode toward the back door.

Seeing the easy-going Cash so determined was a change for me. Usually the man moved slow and casual, like he had nowhere to be and not a care in the world.

Not today.

Today he was a man on a mission and apparently that mission was inspecting my store for intruders.

But no. It was more than that. His real mission was ensuring my safety. And I couldn't lie to myself and deny that his protective side was hot as hell.

I'd wanted the man before, even knowing he was a joker who didn't take much seriously. Now that he was proving me wrong, showing me the other side of the Cash coin, so to speak, my heart was ready to melt.

Heart?

Crap. My lust crush had moved. Up from my lady parts and into the region of my body where real feelings resided.

I didn't want to have real feelings for Cashel Morgan. Not as long as they weren't reciprocal. Not if he didn't have real feelings for me.

Now wasn't the time to be thinking about this because he was standing there yanking on the knob of the back door of my shop hard enough he might tear it off.

"Wait. I have the key."

He glanced over his shoulder, but his two hands remained on the knob. "I know you have the key. Or at least I assumed you did. I'm trying to see how secure this lock is. If someone really wanted to get in, how hard would it be?"

Hard, I hoped, but I wasn't sure.

"It's good that the door opens out," he continued. "At least it can't be kicked in. But they could probably pry it open with a crowbar. Or just pick the lock."

"Who knows how to pick locks around here?" It was Mudville. Not the city.

Cash spun to face me. "Harper. That's who."

"What?" I squeaked.

"Your bestie Harper is apparently well-trained in the use of burglar tools."

"For real?" I asked, still perplexed by the revelation.

"Yup. Stone witnessed it firsthand. Apparently, she whipped out her lock pick set, which she owns by the way, and picked a lock like a pro right in front of him."

"Hmm. That's interesting."

"Stone didn't think it was interesting. It freaked him the fuck out. I never laughed so hard as when he described it to me." Cash chuckled, and then leveled a stare on me. "So, uh, is that key forthcoming or should I actually break in?"

"Oh. Sorry. Yeah. Here it is." I handed over the truck keys, which also held the carriage house key, my apartment door key, and the front door key of the store, as well as the back door. There was another key on there too. I wasn't sure what that one went to but I figured it must be something so I left it on the ring.

Cash stared at the overloaded key ring in his hand then looked back up at me.

"Want me to open it?" I offered.

"Just show me which one it is, please. I want to go inside first. Just in case."

There was that squishy feeling in my heart again.

"Okay."

I managed to reach out and single out the appropriate key. But darn it if I didn't notice how warm his hands were when my skin brushed his. I wanted those hands on me. All over me.

And that would be an epically bad idea. Bad. Bad. Bad.

A person shouldn't poop where they eat. Wasn't that the old saying? Living in a town the size of Mudville meant I couldn't have a one-night stand with anyone. And I really couldn't have a fling with Cash.

He was a Morgan. Everyone in town, and in all the surrounding towns too, knew him and his family. I owned a business, so I wasn't exactly inconspicuous myself.

We were both born and raised here. By all indications, I'd die in this town.

My train of thought was broken by the lights going on in the store after Cash disappeared inside and I still stood outside pondering life and death in a small town.

I had to give Cash credit. He was thorough, searching the shop from top to bottom, including the storage on the third floor. I followed along, answering him as he asked me if everything on each level looked as it should.

Soon we were inside the dark first floor of the carriage house where the store overflow I had stashed there made it nearly impossible to walk through. I had all intentions of eventually fixing up the things in there to sell, but I hadn't gotten to it yet.

Cash didn't comment even though I knew all my stored crap made his job of checking to make sure no one was hiding in there even harder. Eventually he decreed the garage area was safe. That meant it was time to go upstairs. To my apartment. Where my bed was.

I swallowed hard and led the way. He let me, even though he still had my keys in his hand. That little detail made this whole situation feel even weirder.

How many times had I imagined Cash walking me up these stairs? More than I could count. But in none of my imaginings did he push past me to go inside and inspect my home for intruders before he'd allow me past the door.

Finally, he came back to where I stood still waiting and watching his search.

"No boogeymen under the bed." I joked.

"Red . . ." There was a hint of annoyance in his tone.

"I know. I know. I need to take my safety seriously. And I am. I promise."

I just never thought the first time Cashel Morgan was in my apartment it would be to check for burglars behind my shower curtain. I guess my delicate ego had wanted him to be here for other reasons.

"So, does everything look normal to you? Like no one's been in here?"

I pocketed my embarrassment that yes, this mess was typical.

At least, this was how my place looked when I'd flown out of here late for work this morning

I had come home for literally five minutes to change from a T-shirt into a sweater between closing the store and meeting Carson at the bar. Clothes were tossed on the bed, which I hadn't taken the time to make. I knew my toothbrush and toothpaste were still out on the vanity in the bathroom where I'd left them.

And, oh jeez, my Micky and Minnie Mouse

pajamas were hanging on the towel rack in the bathroom where I'd tossed them this morning. Great.

But to answer Cash's question, yes, this was normal. I couldn't blame an intruder for my mess.

"Yeah, everything looks like how I left it."

He nodded slowly, lips pressed tightly as he considered the apartment around us, glancing at the windows then at the door. "I hate to ask this, but any chance you have an alarm on this place? One that actually works."

Unlike the shop, he meant? Point taken. I was lax in security. Though I hated to admit it out loud.

I hesitated. "Um . . ."

"So that's a no." He sighed and I was suddenly torn between guilt and anger over disappointing him. He turned to face me full on. "You have my number, right?"

I frowned. "Um, I'm not sure."

At one time I'd had his number from when he'd helped me deliver some furniture I'd collected to be donated to a family who'd lost their home in a fire. I loved my truck but it didn't fit a queen-sized mattress like Cash's did.

I glanced down at my cell, remembering how I'd bought a new one but hadn't been able to transfer over my contacts. I'd gotten frustrated and given up, thinking I'd do it later. And, as usual, that time had never come.

Without a word, he extended his hand. I didn't need him to tell me what he wanted. I unlocked my phone and handed it over. He punched in his number and handed it back. "You call me if you hear anything tonight. Okay?"

"Yes, sir." My smart-ass comment earned me a raised brow. I smiled, enjoying that I annoyed him as much as he did me. "Thank you, Cash."

"You're welcome." He nodded and stood opposite me.

Awkward . . .

He said, "I guess I'd better get—"

At the same time, I asked, "Did you want something to—"

We spoke over each other, both stopping mid-sentence when we realized what was happening.

"Sorry. You go," I said.

A small smile twitched up his lips. "No, ladies first."

"I was going to ask you if you wanted something to drink. I have um . . . coffee. And I have an old bottle of green crème de menthe from a bunch of years ago. Or tap water." I realized how pitiful my offerings were and cringed.

I really needed to go shopping. I searched my brain for what else I could offer and came up empty.

"Sorry. I don't spend a lot of time here."

He laughed. "It's okay. I should get going anyway."

"Oh. Okay." I stepped aside so he could sidle past me and get out the door.

Cash took a step and then turned back, keys in his hand. "Oops. I almost walked away with your keys."

I laughed. "Well, I can walk to work in the morning so the truck key wouldn't be a problem."

"Yeah." He smiled. "You know, don't ever get rid of that truck without talking to me first."

"Why?" I asked.

"She's a beauty. Besides the fact I'd love to have her, she'd look great at the farm stand. The tourists would love it. Very Instagrammable. Great marketing."

My heart fluttered. Besides my truck, one of my favorite things in the world was talking about marketing. This man was hitting all my buttons.

When I finally found my voice, I asked, "Cashel Morgan, what does a farmer know about marketing?"

"More than you'd think thanks to Dad, whether I like it or not. We'll talk one day. Compare our Pinterest strategies." He grinned.

At what must have been a look of shock on my face, he let out a chuckle and turned to head down the stairs.

Cash lifted one arm in a half-hearted wave on his way down. "G'night, Red."

He didn't turn around as he said it. He just kept walking. But that was okay, because if experience had taught me anything about Cash Morgan, it was that he'd be back.

"Good night, Cash," I replied before he reached the bottom step.

"I'll make sure to close the carriage house door," he said, glancing back at me.

I nodded. "Okay. Thanks."

He held my gaze for a beat too long before breaking eye contact and moving out of my line of sight.

Yup. He'd be back. And this time, I'd be ready.

CHAPTER SIX

Red

The cell phone vibrating on the bedside table finally knocked me out of my slumber.

It took my tired brain a few moments to identify the sound and then set my body into motion to answer it.

With eyes still not quite focused, I blindly swiped at the screen a few times. Finally, I hit the right spot and answered the call from whoever was annoying enough to bother me this early.

Bringing it to my face still squashed in the pillow, I said, "Hello?"

"Are you still sleeping?" Harper demanded through the phone.

"Yes. It's only . . ." I pulled the phone away and squinted at the time on the display. "Seven-thirty-five."

"And you were supposed to pick me up at seven-thirty for the estate sale."

Crud! I'd overslept.

I struggled to sit up. "Oh my God."

"Mm, hm. I knew I should have texted you half an hour ago to make sure you were up." Harper sounded completely and annoyingly awake.

Of course, she was. She probably already had three cups of coffee and had written her daily allotment of words this morning. All while I was still lounging in bed.

As complete opposites, it was amazing we were so close. Maybe that's why we complemented each other so well.

To that point, I said, "Yes, you should have texted."

"Next time I will. Now throw on a baseball hat and start the truck. I'll meet you in the driveway with a cup of coffee in five minutes."

Coffee. Thank God.

"Yes," I hissed. "Bless you! See you then."

Harper knew me well. Knew I looked like a rooster if I didn't shower so it was going to be a baseball hat kind of morning. Also knew nothing was happening, including driving to the sale, until I had caffeine in my body.

We weren't going very far, just to Second Street. It was at the other end of town and the Village of Mudville was only about two miles long.

But I didn't want to be late for this appointment. This was Rose Van de Berg's old house. The infamous Rose, whose lifetime worth of journals had rocked this village and all our lives last year when Harper and I discovered them in an old trunk in Agnes's attic.

The old lady had died, childless, twenty years ago at the age of ninety-nine. Her heirs had sold the house on the acre of land immediately, fully furnished. An older man from the city had bought it and had put on a modern addition, which is where he mostly lived. As far as I knew, he'd pretty much left the original part of the structure and furnishings intact.

All things came full circle and that owner had died too. History was repeating itself and his heirs were selling the house and property in its entirety. They'd hired a local estate sale company to handle everything and luckily, I was friends with the owner of that company.

I was getting the first look—or at least the second look after Joan—of the original contents of Rose Van de Berg's house. More importantly, the attic, where all good things were always found.

Joan was letting me inside a full three hours before the public would be allowed in and I didn't want to miss a minute of that time. Who knew what treasures we'd find? Or what secrets.

"I can't believe today of all days you overslept." Harper cocked a brow as she stood next to my truck, two cups of coffee in her hands and a judgmental expression on her face.

I unlocked the passenger side of the truck for her and I happily accepted the cup she handed me. I took a big sip of hot liquid before moving to the other side of the truck and making my apology.

"I know. Believe me. I want to get into that house even more than you do."

What could I say to Harper? She was right. Of all days to oversleep, today was the worst.

At least I had an excuse. "I didn't sleep well last night."

I hesitated to tell her what had happened last night with the guy Cash had seen creeping around my yard, which was crazy. She'd know exactly how I felt.

She'd been in bed when the guy broke into Agnes's house. He was up in the attic, actually inside the house with her. But I didn't want that topic to consume this morning.

It really could have just been a kid cutting through the yard. Lord knows I'd taken plenty of shortcuts when I was a kid trying to get home before curfew. In the end I started the truck, thanked her for the coffee, and left it at that.

"What do you think we'll find in there?" she asked, looking as excited as I felt.

"Who knows? It could be anything. Rose was born in that house—like literally born in one of the bedrooms. Her father had the house built as a wedding gift for her mother. There could be stuff from the turn of the last century inside. That house is a piece of Mudville history."

"Wow," Harper breathed. "And it's the last owner who stuck that modern addition on it?"

"Yup." I nodded but left it at that without further commentary.

She cut me a sideways glance. "Go on. You can say it. *Fucking city folk.*"

I laughed as Harper did a great imitation of Stone's favorite refrain. It had been a source of conflict between the two of them back before they started dating, when Harper was the *city girl* that local farmer Stone was railing against.

"Not all city folk are created equal," I said, and added, "And yes, I know. You're not from the city. But *suburban folk* doesn't have quite the same ring to it." I grinned.

"Yeah, I know. Sad but true, I have to agree with that." She sighed.

I pulled into the driveway, arriving at the house before the truck even had a chance to really warm up enough for me to turn on the heat. "We're here."

Harper leaned forward to get a better look at the house through the windshield. "I can't believe I didn't know this was Rose's old house."

I glanced at her as I cut the ignition. "You only officially moved to Mudville when? Not even two months ago. Give yourself a break. You can't know everything."

"But I like knowing everything," she joked, opening the passenger door with a loud screeching creak.

"You always are an over-achiever." I laughed at her as I made a mental note that I needed to oil that hinge. Antique trucks needed love . . . and occasionally WD-40.

"Only-child syndrome. I can't help it." She said

before stepping out.

I slammed my door and met her on the other side of the truck. We both stood in front of the blue octagon-shaped house that sat on the bank of the Muddy River.

"There used to be a gazebo here," I said as I gazed at the facade. "I've seen pictures."

If you didn't look behind the original house at the addition you could almost picture the turn of the century garden parties that no doubt took place on the home's sweeping front lawn.

"That must have been beautiful."

"Yeah," I agreed, then knocked myself out of my nostalgia and into work mode. Joan's car was already there, so I knew we could get inside. "Come on. Let's get in there and see what the damn city folk left for us to find."

She raised a brow but didn't argue. We were both too excited to get inside.

Joan was busy as heck getting ready for the sale, so after a quick introduction to Harper, she gave us a pack of stickers and free rein to explore. All I had to do was put a sticker on anything I wanted to buy and then settle up with her and move the stuff out later.

My heart was pounding as Harper stood in the center hall, looking left and then right. "Where to first?"

"The attic, of course." I led the way, barreling up the stairs.

"Why is it always the attic?" she asked from

behind me.

I glanced back before turning the corner of the grand center staircase. "Because I know you love attics so much," I joked, knowing the opposite was true.

She groaned.

But I actually did have a good reason to head to the attic first. The Muddy River had flooded this town not once but twice over the past hundred years. The basement and first floor would have been affected, but not the attic. That's where a smart homeowner who lived riverfront would keep their best stuff stored.

As we made our way to the third floor, winded from our sprint up the stairs, I hoped my theory proved true. When we reached the attic door my heart was pounding as much with anticipation as from the exertion.

Hand on the knob, I glanced back at Harper. "Ready?" I asked.

She beamed. "Never been more ready."

"All right. Let's see what other secrets Rose left us." I had to admit my hand trembled a bit as I turned the old knob and pushed.

It took me forcing it open with my shoulder but finally the door let loose and we were faced with a century's worth of dust and underneath it, a lifetime's worth of memories.

"Oh my God. It's like a time capsule." Harper stepped inside the cavernous space swirling with dust in the beams of sunlight streaming through the windows.

I didn't know where to look first. I whipped out the flashlight I'd remembered to stick in my jeans pocket and headed for the piles of stuff in one dark corner.

"Look at this old croquet set," Harper exclaimed from the other side of the attic.

"Put a sticker on it," I called back as I did the same to an old oil portrait leaned up against the wall. The frame alone was worth money, but if I could identify the subject of the painting as being one of the founding members of this town, it would be even more valuable.

"There's a trunk here," Harper said. "It looks almost like the one we found in Agnes's attic."

"Open it," I said, climbing over some chairs to put a sticker on an old wooden cradle that looked handmade and well over a hundred years old. "Maybe it's more journals."

"It can't possibly be more journals, could it?" There was a pause and then Harper said, "Wow."

At her exclamation, my head whipped up from where I'd uncovered a box of some old—as in really old—records. The kind that worked on the old Edison or Victrola players. And where there were records, there should be the player as well.

"Wow what?" I nearly fell flat on my face scrambling over the pile of wooden stacked folding chairs to get to Harper.

I couldn't see what she was looking at since the trunk and its open lid blocked my view. It wasn't until

I was next to her that I saw it. A wedding dress, carefully folded and stored in the trunk for I didn't know how long.

I wiped my hands on the legs of my jeans to clean off any dirt and reached inside. I gently lifted the fabric, very aware that this dress could be over a hundred and twenty years old if it belonged to Rose's mother. But when I lifted it, I could tell by the styling it wasn't Victorian. But it could be Depression era.

"I wonder who it belonged to." Harper glanced at me.

"I don't know. It's the right time period to be Rose's, but I thought she was never married."

"No. She was. Remember when Margaret Trout broke into Agnes's to look for Rose's journals too, after Joe broke in?"

"How could I forget?" I snorted.

"She told me Agnes was widowed very young. What if they were married and he died in the first war?"

I could see her mind working, spinning tales of possibilities and romance.

"There was nothing in her journals about her husband though, was there?" I asked.

"No." She looked disappointed.

I didn't worry too much about her. What she didn't find she'd make up and put in her next book. I had no doubt.

"Are you going to buy the dress?" she asked.

"I don't really sell vintage clothes, or wedding

gowns." When she looked sad about that, I said, "You want it?"

"Can I? Am I allowed?" she asked, wide eyed.

"Sure. You're with me. I'll put a sticker on it for you."

What she was going to do with a wedding dress, of unknown size, from World War I, was beyond me, but who was I to judge? I'd bought stranger things at estate sales, to keep for myself, not to sell.

I put the dress back and pressed a sticker to the fabric inside the neckline. We'd spent enough time speculating about the dress's owner. There was still so much to search through.

Happy that she had her dress secured, Harper had moved on to the other side of the attic.

Divide and conquer—between the two of us we should be able to get through everything before the public sale started.

"Huh."

Or maybe we wouldn't get through it all if I kept running over to see what she was exclaiming about.

"What?" I asked, pausing in my search for that antique record player I was convinced was in here somewhere.

She turned to me. "Didn't you say you lost a buffalo plaid cape at the shop?"

"Yeah." Had she found a vintage plaid cape? If she did, that thing was so mine.

"Like this one?" She bent down and when she straightened, I saw what she held in her hands.

It didn't look vintage. In fact, it looked exactly like the one I'd lost.

I moved over to where she stood and used my flashlight to look at the tag.

"This is the same brand as the one from my shop." The one that had gone missing. "Where did you find it?"

"Right there on the floor. On top of that Coleman sleeping bag."

"Sleeping bag." In an attic filled with more than a century of dusty old furniture, a new cape and modern sleeping bag stood out like a sore thumb. I moved the beam of my flashlight to the sleeping bag and gasped. "That's from my shop too."

"Really? How do you know?"

"That's my price tag on it." My eyes widened as I realized this was what had looked wrong downstairs when I'd searched the store to see if anything besides the cape was missing. I couldn't put my finger on it then, but now it was obvious.

"What is this stuff from your store doing here?" she asked.

"I don't know. But I sure as heck would like to find out."

After that discovery, the excitement of the sale shifted. I couldn't concentrate on antiques knowing that I wasn't crazy. Someone had been in my shop. Things had been taken.

A certain amount of theft was a given when you owned a store, but this felt different. It wasn't simple shoplifting.

"I have to call the sheriff," I murmured, more to myself than to Harper.

"You definitely do," she agreed. "Something is going on in this town."

Her eyes widened when she turned back to me.

"And this is Rose's old house." Open mouthed she shook her head. "Again, that woman is smack in the middle of a Mudville mystery. Twenty years after she died."

Harper was doing what she did best, taking tidbits and spinning them into stories, but I couldn't argue with her.

She was right.

Something was happening in Mudville. Something mysterious. Whether it involved Rose again or not was yet to be determined. But, like it or not, it seemed I was somehow smack in the middle of it this time.

CHAPTER SEVEN

Cash

"Mother fucker!" I slowed and narrowed my eyes at the deputy vehicle parked in Red's lot. Again.

Jaw clenched, I swung my truck down the side street.

This was my own damn fault. I'd told her about the guy sneaking around her yard. And I'd been dumb enough to not call the sheriff and I'd admitted that to her.

Of course, she would call herself. Even though I had told her I'd handle it this morning, which was exactly what I was on my way to do.

The sheriff at her place was just proof she didn't trust me to keep my word.

That pissed me off. Until another thought hit. What if this had nothing to do with the creeper in her yard and everything to do with her *date,* or whatever it was that she had with Carson last night?

Fuck. That scenario was even worse than her not trusting me to report the incident.

Whatever was going on, I wasn't going to let it happen without me being there.

After cutting the engine and yanking the key out of the ignition, I swung my door wide. I stepped down and glared at the deputy car, parked crooked next to me.

It would serve him right if I slammed my door right into his car after the shitty way he'd parked.

Carson must've been in a real hurry to get inside to see Red.

Angry, annoyed, and full of adrenaline, I took the front stairs two at a time and strode through the front door of the shop.

There, as expected, I got a look at Carson and Red looking cozy, their heads bent close together so they almost touched. His hand was on her hand as they both looked at something on her cell phone.

Seriously, what the fuck was happening right now?

I cleared my throat when they didn't bother to even look up, in spite of the jingling bell and the fact I'd slammed the door pretty hard behind me.

"Cash," Red breathed with an air of excitement when she finally glanced up.

What had her so breathless and excited? The good deputy?

At that thought my breakfast of bacon and eggs churned in my gut.

"Red," I returned her greeting, then unhappily moved my gaze to the man standing much too closely to her. "Carson."

He nodded. "Cash."

I swallowed. "So, uh, what's up?"

I kept my tone casual, so it didn't reveal what I was really thinking. That being, what the fuck was he doing practically embracing Red in public, in her shop during business hours? Not that I'd have preferred him to do it after hours and in private, but I had to deal with the situation at hand.

"Remember that buffalo plaid cape that was missing?" she asked.

Buffalo plaid. I wasn't even sure I knew what exactly buffalo plaid was.

"The cape I thought was lost but might have been stolen?" she continued.

"Yeah." I remembered the conversation.

It was the whole reason for Carson being here yesterday. Also the reason for the police report that just *had* to be delivered in person at Lainey's bar over hot wings last night.

Red reached down and then tossed something that was red and black onto the counter. "I found it."

That was buffalo plaid? Just big red and black checks? Why not just freaking say that?

Accepting that I had no control over the world and its oddities, I said, "All right. Good, you found it. So it wasn't stolen."

"Not exactly." Good old Carson chimed into the conversation, just when I'd been ignoring him.

"I found it in Rose's attic." Wide eyed, Red looked at me as if that should mean something.

I felt the frown settle on my forehead. "Old lady Rose who's been dead for like twenty years?"

"Yes!" she squealed, looking excited.

"I'm confused." I shook my head.

Carson drew in a breath. "Rose's house is being sold by the estate of the last owner. There's a big public sale there today. Red was over there for a preview this morning. The cape was in the attic along with another item from her store."

"In the middle of all the century old stuff in the dusty old attic was this cape and a Coleman sleeping bag with my price tag still on it. And an empty can of beans. I was showing Carson the pictures of where I found it all in Rose's old attic."

"It's good she took the pictures. The sale already started and once the public gets in there any evidence will be tainted," Carson added.

I was beginning to understand her agitation, even as I breathed a sigh of relief that Carson was supposedly on top of her just to see the photos.

"Rose's old place was owned by an out-of-towner. It was empty most of the year," I commented, putting the pieces together.

Carson nodded. "Correct. The owner died. Joan from the estate sale company was the first one inside in months."

"It sounds like a squatter to me. He needed something warm so he grabbed the sleeping bag and that wool thing to use as a blanket. But that doesn't make me feel any better that this person, whoever it was, broke into your store."

"I've been thinking about that. I wonder if they were in here while I was open. Then just hid until after I locked up. They could help themselves to anything they wanted and then sneak out the back door, locking it behind them. They probably thought I wouldn't notice. And you know what? If it wasn't for that specific cape, I probably wouldn't have."

I liked that scenario better than thinking someone was able to break in, but I did not like the thought of Red closing up here, alone, with someone hiding inside.

"That doesn't explain who was here last night though," I said.

"Wait? What's this now?" Carson asked. "Someone was here again last night?"

I smothered my cringe. "I was actually on my way to the department to make a report. I spotted someone creeping around by the shop's back door last night. I got out of the truck and went after him, but he ran."

"You keep saying *he*. Are you sure the suspect was a male?" Carson asked.

Knee-jerk reaction was to say yes, but now that I thought about it, I really wasn't certain. In fact, the shadowy figure wasn't large. It was on the smaller side. It could have been a female or even a young teen maybe.

"No, I'm not sure," I admitted. "I really didn't get a good look."

Carson had his pad out and was jotting down notes. "What time was this?"

That was easy. I remembered exactly. "What time did Red meet you at Lainey's?"

He frowned. "Why does that matter?"

Because I saw her walk in and couldn't get out of there fast enough, that's why.

I kept that truth to myself and instead said, "I remember seeing her walk in on my way out. I was heading home when I spotted the figure by her shop and turned down her side street."

My little white lie, or stretching of the truth, should hold up if he didn't try to poke holes in it. And even if he did, there was no way in hell I was going to admit I was staking out Red's place to see if she brought him home with her.

"Anything else you can remember?" Carson, thankfully, accepted my answer without further question and moved on after jotting down something more in his tiny book.

I felt like we were in some black and white film. I guess the Mudville sheriff's department didn't believe in using the note app on their cell phones.

"Nope. That's about it," I said, hating that, archaic writing devices aside, Carson actually seemed pretty good at his job.

"All right." He flipped his little notebook closed and shoved it into his pocket, glancing down at Red. "I'll go back to Rose's and see if I can find anything else when the crowds clear.

"Great. Thanks. I really appreciate all your help."

"My pleasure." Carson grinned.

I'm sure it was his pleasure. I controlled the grumble of a groan as Carson glanced up at me. "See you around, Cash."

"Yeah. See you." *Goodbye and good riddance.*

Finally, when the distracting presence that was the deputy was gone, Red turned to me. "You just stopping by to check on me or did you need something?"

I needed her to stop hanging out with Carson. But besides that, I was good.

Dammit. Why couldn't I come up with a single reason to be here besides the obvious, that I was checking up on her and Carson?

"Um, just making sure you were okay. After last night with the guy or whoever. I wanted to make sure you're all right."

"Thank you, Cash. That's sweet."

Sweet. I evaluated how that word made me feel. Was being sweet a good thing? Didn't nice guys finish last?

In my experience, sweet guys hooked up the girl's security system while the other guy got the date at the bar. Sweet guys sat in a cold dark truck and waited to make sure the girl got home safely, while she called the other guy the next morning.

I didn't want to be the good guy. I wanted to be bad. To back Red up into that work room and kiss her breathless. I wanted to sweep the junk off her desk, set her up there and pound both of us into a screaming orgasm.

"So, um . . ." Red hesitated, which was intriguing. If there was one thing this woman could do to excess it was talk.

I waited, brows raised expectantly. I was always interested in what she had to say, but now even more so, given how oddly reluctant she was to spill whatever it was.

Finally, she continued, "Would you like to have dinner at my place tonight?"

My eyes popped wide. Of all the things I might have guessed she would say, that wasn't one of them.

"Really?"

Shit. What the fuck was that answer?

I should just say yes. *Hell, yes. What time? Let's eat now.* Instead I questioned her? Jesus.

"Yeah," she continued. "I mean, you did so much work for me on the cameras and would only accept a cup of coffee for it. I would have bought you a beer last night at the bar, but you left so fast. And then you took all that time to walk through with me last night after you saw that person in my yard. I want to thank you properly."

Not one to make the same mistake twice, I pocketed anything else I might have wanted to say about that and instead nodded. "Yes. I'd love to. What time?"

"Um, six?"

"What can I bring?"

"Nothing. Just yourself."

"You sure?" I asked.

"Yup." She nodded. "Gretchen comes in at two-thirty today so I'll be able to sneak out early and get everything ready."

"Don't go to any trouble for me."

Crap. I really was incapable of just letting things go, wasn't I? Before I knew it, I'd end up accidentally talking her out of the whole dinner idea.

I needed to keep my mouth shut and be grateful.

A whole night alone with Red in her apartment. That was even better than hot wings at the bar. My date with her would beat Carson's hands down.

Though this was a thank-you dinner. Not a date.

Fuck it. I didn't care. When it came to Red, I'd take anything I could get.

CHAPTER EIGHT

Red

"Can you fit me in for a quick trim?" I asked, skidding to a stop on the linoleum floor of Ruby's hair salon.

I was out of breath since I'd almost sprinted here the moment Gretchen had arrived for her shift. The beauty shop was just two short blocks away, so I didn't take the truck.

Frowning, Ruby took in my breathless, frantic state. "Sure. I've got no one scheduled for another hour."

"Oh, thank God," I breathed, more to myself than to her.

Cash had just seen me this morning so why getting my hair done before dinner seemed so important, I didn't know, but it did.

Smiling, she said, "Wish all my customers were that grateful. Take a seat at the sink."

"Thanks." I tossed my purse on an empty chair and sat in front of the washing sink.

"What's the occasion?" she asked, tying a cape around my neck before she reached back to start the water.

I hadn't been expecting that question. Though I suppose I shouldn't have run in here like I was desperate if I wanted to pretend this was just a routine haircut.

"No occasion," I lied. "You know how it is. Short hair looks great when it's first cut and has shape. Then one day you wake up and can't do a thing with it. I'm starting to look like a little boy with bed head, no matter what I try to do with it."

Most of that was the truth. I was overdue for a haircut and I'd developed a strange cowlick that I couldn't tame in spite of how much hair product I used.

The only thing I was guilty of was a lie of omission. That the urgency stemmed from my sudden date with Cash tonight. If I could call it a date.

Dinner. That's all it was. Just two friends having dinner.

As my heart pounded at the thought, I forced a smile and decided to change the subject. "So, what's up with you since I saw you last?"

If there was one thing Ruby was good at, besides cutting hair, it was talking. And Mudville, even with as small as it was, gave her plenty to talk about. Enough to carry us through my wash, cut and blow dry.

After I paid and left a generous tip for her squeezing me in, I was off again. I ran into the grocery store on Main Street and picked up a few of the things I'd need for tonight's dinner. I dropped that bag at home, sticking the cold stuff in the fridge and grabbed the truck keys.

My next errand was too far to walk. I was taking a trip to the farm. Morgan Farm, where there was a good chance I'd run into at least one Morgan family member, whether I wanted to or not.

The farm stand wouldn't open until spring when the first crops started coming in from the field, but the farm had a little shop—if you could call the eight by ten foot shed that—which they left unmanned and open to the public year-round.

Inside was a freezer unit filled with meat from their cattle and a refrigerator with milk from their dairy cows.

Only in a small town would you find this kind of set-up.

There was a counter with a ledger book and a pen and a cash box. Customers wrote down what they took and how much it cost in the book, next to the date and their name, then shoved their cash for the items into the slot in the locked box that was attached to the counter. All on the honor system.

It always amazed me, being in retail myself and having experienced more than my share of items walking away right out from under my nose. But the Morgans made it work. I guess what they'd have to pay for an employee to man the little shop would cost far more than what the few dishonest people walked off with.

In any case, I knew I couldn't feed Cash a steak

from the grocery store or give him commercial brand milk for our coffee either, for that matter.

I drew in a breath and parked my truck by the shed, hoping that Cash wouldn't be inside stocking the freezer or whatever. It would feel too weird seeing him now as I ran around like a chicken with no head trying to prepare for our dinner together.

Pulling open the door, I was faced with a broad back and stopped dead in the doorway. I considered going back out but it was too late. He'd no doubt have heard the door.

My heart pounding, I waited to be faced with Cash as I bought the steak and cream-line milk for . . . whatever this was. Date. Dinner. I didn't know, but I wasn't prepared to decide at this very moment.

I froze and watched him turn around . . . and finally could breathe again when I saw not Cash, but his older brother Stone.

Dressed in the heavy Carhart jacket and knit hat, it was impossible to tell the brothers apart from behind.

"Hey, Red."

Trying to calm my racing pulse, I said, "Hey, Stone. What's up?"

"Not much. Just restocking."

I noticed the steaks in the crate he held. "Those frozen yet? I need something for dinner tonight."

Grabbing fresh steaks would save me having to defrost them before tonight's dinner.

"Nope. You need one?" he asked.

"Uh, two actually."

"Hungry? Or are you having company?" he asked, one brow raised.

When did Stone become such a conversationalist?

He used to be the king of one-word answers. Now, when I was trying to avoid telling him about Cash coming over, he was suddenly all chatty?

I chose to blame Harper's influence on Stone for this new inquisitiveness as I scrambled to come up with an excuse. "I might have company."

"Not Harper, right? Because I was planning on having dinner with her tonight."

"No. Not Harper. Uh, Bethany. She's been feeling kind of down in the dumps lately. You know, with you and Harper all paired off." I lifted one shoulder, nonchalantly throwing my friend under the bus with the lie.

Stone frowned, apparently not liking the imaginary blame I'd thrown on him.

Good. Maybe his displeasure would keep him occupied until I grabbed two steaks and a quart of milk and got the heck out of here. Hopefully before Cash walked in too. Or, just as bad, their youngest brother Boone, who always did like to chat and ask a lot of questions.

Stepping forward, I grabbed the top two steaks from Stone's box, while fumbling for the cash I'd shoved in my pocket after my haircut.

Meanwhile, Stone had gone silent. Perfect. I grabbed my milk and scribbled my purchase on the list before shoving the bills into the box.

After a quick goodbye to Stone, I headed out the door.

Mission accomplished. I'd made a clean getaway.

Starting the truck, which actually turned over right away without any hesitation, my next stop was home.

But crud! I still needed dessert. Lucky for me Bethany's was still open. This impromptu dinner was a lot of work.

I pulled up along the curb on Main Street and parked in front of her bakery, prepared to face one more challenge. Was she in there or one of her employees? Bethany might ask questions if I was there buying a bunch of desserts.

Afraid I'd used up my good luck for the day at Morgan's, I held my breath and pushed open the door.

"Hey!" Bethany greeted, happy to see me. I wished I could say the same about me seeing her.

"Hey. Um, so what's good?" I asked, approaching the glass case.

"Everything is good, but if you're asking if there's anything special today, then yes. I'm trying out these new individual -sized red velvet cheesecakes and they came out amazing. And I've got heart shaped butter cookies dipped in white chocolate. I stenciled fun messages on them, like those candy message hearts people buy. They're going to be perfect for Valentine's Day."

"Yeah. They will be. That sounds good. I'll take a couple of both."

"Okay. Should I wrap up one of each for you to go or are you going to eat here?" she asked.

Here we go. More lying. "Uh, can you wrap it? And actually, I'll take two of the cookies and the cheesecake."

She glanced up at me. "Two of even the cheesecake? They're pretty big."

"Yeah. That's okay. I'm gonna, uh, bring one back to Gretchen." I was weaving myself quite the web of little white lies today and I had a bad feeling it was going to all come back and bite me in the butt.

Hopefully, Stone wouldn't tell Harper that I'd said I was having dinner with Bethany. If Harper brought it up to Bethany, I'd be caught. And I'd be just as caught if Bethany came into the shop and asked Gretchen how she'd liked the new red velvet cheesecake.

I sighed. I really was a horrible liar. But it couldn't be avoided if I didn't want anyone—make that *everyone* since news traveled fast in this town—to know I was having dinner with Cash.

But really, why did it matter?

I knew the answer to that. Harper, Bethany, even Stone, would make assumptions about us having dinner together. I was too confused about what Cash and I were or were not to each other already.

If my friends knew I liked Cash that way, they'd keep asking questions and harping on it. Looking too deeply into every time I even talked to him or about him.

It was too much pressure.

Yes, I wanted more with him. But if he didn't want that too, and we ended up just staying friends, I'd deal with it. I'd rather do that privately. Without an audience, even if they were my best friends.

Bethany handing me the white bakery box tied with red and white string interrupted my inner dialogue. "Anything else?"

"Nope. That's it. Thanks. I'd better get back to the store."

Please don't ask what I'm doing tonight. Please. Please. Please. I chanted that plea silently as I handed her the money.

Bethany smiled and said, "Okay. Enjoy."

Phew. That was it. No questions. I could go.

"Thanks. I will." I might have sprinted out of the bakery, making my escape a bit faster than necessary, but my adrenaline was running on high.

Good thing I'd forgotten to order a coffee to go. I obviously didn't need the caffeine.

But so far, so good. My errands were done and my secret was still intact.

Now I could move on to my next worry. What the heck was I going to wear tonight for my possible but most likely not-a-date date?

I had no idea and probably nothing in my closet.

Good thing I owned a store.

CHAPTER NINE

Cash

"Where are you going?"

I stopped at the sound of Boone's voice, my hand on the doorknob of the kitchen.

Crap. So close.

I'd almost made it out of the house without encountering either of my brothers. You'd think they'd have something better to do than hang around the kitchen catching me sneaking out.

Morgan Farm didn't run itself. Though sometimes it seemed that way with the amount of time Boone and Stone had free to butt their noses in my business.

"Out," I said, hoping my little brother would accept that answer.

"Out where?" Stone walked into the room, obviously hearing the conversation from the hallway.

I got a look at the odd, almost amused expression on Stone's face. He looked like more of a smart ass than usual. Not at all like his regular grumpy self.

In fact, he was acting a bit like me. What the fuck?

"What does it matter where?" I asked.

"Well, Mom made a nice dinner and it's gonna be on the table in about half an hour, so I thought it would be nice if you stuck around to eat it," Stone informed me.

"I told Mom I'm going out, so don't worry about it." I narrowed my eyes at Stone.

He was in his good clothes. And his hair was damp, like he'd just showered. And he smelled like cologne.

Mother fucker. He was going out too. Yet he was giving me shit about doing the same thing?

I folded my arms and glared at him. "Looks to me like you're going to miss Mom's dinner too."

Boone frowned and turned to sweep Stone with a full body glance. "You're going out too? Am I the only one not going out tonight?"

"Looks like." Stone nodded to Boone and then turned to me. "And for your information, I have a zoning board meeting."

"You got all dressed up for Mayor Picket and the old biddies in town?" *Doubtful.*

"No, I did not. I'm having a late dinner with Harper after the meeting's over, but we're talking about you now." Stone folded his arms across his chest.

"What *about* me?" I scowled.

"About where *you* are going without *me*." Boone cocked up a brow, looking most unhappy to be the only one left home with Mom and Dad.

"I think I know." Stone grinned. "At least I have a good guess."

"Oh, do you now? What do you think you know?" I asked, cocky and confident he didn't know shit.

There was no way Stone knew where I was going. I hadn't mentioned a word to anyone. I'd gone about my chores for the day without saying a thing about dinner or anything else.

"You're having dinner at Red's."

I almost choked at his eerily accurate guess.

It didn't help my discomposure when Boone turned to me grinning. "Now that makes a whole lot of sense."

Recovering enough to respond I asked them both, "Why does it make sense? And why in the world do you think I'm doing something with Red tonight?"

"Do you need me to remind you about how you looked when she walked into the bar to have dinner with Carson the other night?" Boone asked.

"Oh really? You'll have to tell me all about that, Boone." Stone lifted a brow. "As for tonight, Red came in and bought two huge steaks and told me she was having dinner with Bethany. But Bethany told me she's going to be at the zoning meeting and hadn't heard anything about dinner but that Red had been in today to buy a bunch of desserts from her."

That was quite a steaming pile of circumstantial evidence my brothers had. But no actual proof as far as I was concerned.

"When did you take over Mary Brimley's duties as town gossip?" I asked Stone.

"He *is* dating a romance novelist," Boone pointed out.

That earned Boone a quick glare from Stone before he turned to me. "I don't hear you denying you have a date with Red tonight."

I sighed. There might be only one way to shut them up. The truth.

"It's not a date. I did some work for her at the shop. She's thanking me with dinner. That's all."

Stone smirked. "Yeah. Harper *thanked* me with dinner after I did her a favor once too. Look where that led."

I folded my arms over my chest. "I'm not as susceptible to a pretty face as you are."

"Now he's calling Red pretty." Boone grinned. "No doubt about it. Cash has a crush on Red."

Jesus. Things had gone from bad to worse. I turned toward the door and said, "I'm going."

"Night, Cash. See you in the morning," Boone said pointedly.

"Walk of shame should happen around dawn. I'll make sure I'm up for it," Stone added.

"Cool, I'll join you. Make the coffee if you get down here before me," Boone added.

My fucking brothers . . . I swear. Sometimes it was like they were twelve.

I bit the inside of my cheek until I tasted blood to

stop from answering them. Responding would have only added fuel to the fire.

They didn't need any encouragement to be juvenile. And I needed to get out of there before I lost the tenuous hold I had on my cool.

It was early to be leaving for Red's but fuck it. I'd rather hang out on her block in the truck than stay here for more abuse from my sophomoric siblings.

I heard their laughs and continued jokes behind me. Being the stronger man, I kept walking, selectively deaf when it came to idiots. Call it a skill I'd perfected from a lifetime of having brothers.

It was the time of year that the sun set early, so it was dark when I pulled down Red's side street at five-thirty.

The shop was still open for business, but I assumed Gretchen was closing tonight since I could see Red's lights on in her apartment above the carriage house. She must be home getting ready for our . . . our what?

Dinner felt like a nice safe generic description for tonight's activities.

A dinner could be anything. There were friendly dinners. Business dinners. Thank-you dinners.

There were any number of reasons for two people to have a friendly meal together that didn't have anything to do with it being a date.

No doubt, Red and I were friends.

We had been since kindergarten when the teacher had sat us alphabetically. Having the name Morgan put me right behind Rebecca Meyer, though I don't think I ever heard anyone except that teacher on the first day of class call Red by her given name.

The little strawberry blonde fireball had stood up, planted her fists on her hips and corrected Mrs. Parson on day one with enough attitude the poor woman never made the mistake of calling her Rebecca again.

I smiled at the memory of a young fiery Red as I glanced at the time on the dash.

Yup. Still too early to knock on her door.

I sighed and glanced at the shop—the answer to how best to kill half an hour or so would be to check out if Red had gotten in anything interesting lately.

Yeah, that was a good plan. The really good stuff sold fast so it never hurt to keep checking.

I usually did my checking when I knew Red was working, but today a little shopping while she wasn't around would serve my purposes of killing time nicely.

But as I stepped through the entrance, I heard Red before I saw her. She was talking to someone upstairs. Or rather she was complaining, loud enough for me to hear downstairs. Something about inconsistency in sizing.

"Jeepers. Even boots in my usual size don't fit me anymore in the calves. It's not like I gained fifty pounds. I swear I only gained like five—maybe seven pounds. And that's all Bethany's fault for making me taste all those recipes for her blog—"

I knew she'd been coming down the stairs just

from the sound of her stomping and her voice getting progressively louder. But the sight of her coming around that corner and seeing me standing there was priceless.

"Red." I grinned.

Her big blue eyes flew wide. Her porcelain skin colored with a pretty blush and she froze on the bottom step. "Cash. Um, hi."

"Hi." I took a step closer, realizing her position put her eye level with me now, when she was usually a head shorter.

Perfect height for kissing . . . if she and I did that sort of thing.

And why didn't we do that sort of thing?

With her looking so tempting, I couldn't think of a single reason why not.

Did that big pink sweater she was wearing over faded jeans and knee-high tan suede boots feel as soft as it looked?

I knocked the image of wrapping Red in my arms and kissing that shocked little mouth of hers out of my head, for now, saving it to be reconsidered later.

"Sorry, I'm a little early," I said.

Gretchen came around the bend in the stairs, loaded down with an arm full of clothes and shoes. Her face lit with a smile when she saw me. "Early for what? Your *date*?"

"Dinner," Red and I both corrected Gretchen at the same time.

Red continued, "It's just a dinner."

I wasn't sure if I should be insulted or not that she was making the extra effort to make sure it was completely clear to this high schooler who worked for her part time that we were *not* on a date.

Of course, maybe that was my fault. I sure as hell wasn't acting like this was a date. I should have brought something. At least a six-pack, or even a bottle of wine.

I restrained an eye-roll at myself. A six-pack of beer from the gas station was not exactly romantic.

But this wasn't supposed to be romantic. It was a thank-you dinner.

How many times had I repeated that same thing to myself? How come it wasn't sticking?

My head was spinning with it all. I decided to do the one thing I'd wanted to since I saw her walk into view. Tell her how great she looked.

"You look really nice. Cozy. Which is good. It's getting pretty cold out there."

"Don't worry. I've got the heater on over at my apartment."

Shit. I'd insulted her.

I didn't want her to think I was assuming eating dinner at her place would require extra sweaters just because she lived above the carriage house.

She only lived there because she'd chosen to turn her entire house into retail space. I had huge respect for her opening the shop all on her own.

My family ran a farm stand an eighth of the size of hers and there were a whole bunch of us who shared the duties. She was doing this alone.

I scrambled to correct her misconception. "I'm sure it'll be real toasty. You ready to head over?"

I did not tell her that I was in such a hurry to get to her place partially because I wasn't a big fan of heaters running when nobody was home. From volunteering for the Mudville Fire Department since I was sixteen, I'd responded to too many fires caused by space heaters.

"Uh, yeah." She glanced at Gretchen. "You going to be—"

"I'll be fine." Gretchen tossed the things she'd been holding on the counter and physically grabbed Red's shoulders to turn her toward the door. "Go. I can close up here alone. I've done it before."

"I know. Just making sure." Red hesitated as her gaze shot from Gretchen, to me, then back again.

Was Red nervous? I wasn't sure how I felt about that.

But truth be told I was feeling a little out of sorts about tonight too. All the more reason to get the night started. We could probably both use a drink to relax.

With that thought in mind, I asked, "You have beer? I can run and pick up some."

"You're good. I bought some," she said as she walked out the door ahead of me.

"Okay. Great. Still, I should have thought to bring some."

"Stop. This is a thank-you dinner. You did the

work. I provide the dinner. That includes beer."

Independent to the core, she was.

I smiled. "All right. I accept. Thank you."

"My pleasure. Hope you're hungry. I've got steak with fried mushrooms and onions and mashed potatoes. And I picked up dessert from Bethany's."

"Sounds good," I said.

And it did. That was no lie.

But as I watched Red climb the stairs to her apartment ahead of me, I had to admit something. While I was definitely looking forward to tonight, I was pretty sure it had nothing to do with the food.

CHAPTER TEN

Red

The night was going well, I guess.

It would have been better if I wasn't a nervous wreck, but what could I do about that?

I didn't dare have a third beer. I was clumsy on a good day stone cold sober. Another one and I might end up spilling the coffee in Cash's lap.

Although then he'd have to take his pants off . . .

Jeez. I was a lunatic around this man.

It was like I forgot how to flirt. But maybe I never did know how to act like a real woman around Cash.

With him I was more a school chum. Like one of the guys. The girl he'd picked for his team in dodge ball because he knew I could both throw and catch.

I was most definitely in the friend zone.

That had been fine in grade school. It had stopped being fine in fifth grade when I fully realized my schoolgirl crush on him. It was definitely not okay now that I was an adult woman.

I had adult feelings. I also had adult needs. Needs I'd love Cash to take care of.

But then what? Was one incredible night with him worth the lifetime of awkwardness that would follow?

How did people do it? Have a casual hook up in a town the size of Mudville where you were pretty much guaranteed to see the other person daily until one of you died?

It was quite the conundrum.

Conundrum.

That was the word-of-the-day last week in the calendar Bethany had given me for Christmas as a joke gift, but not really a joke, because Harper was always using words that Bethany and I had to look up.

My mind was spinning. I could blame Cash for that. He was very distracting in his tight long-sleeved T-shirt. The way it outlined his upper body and all those hard-earned muscles.

Throwing bales of hay and splitting cords of firewood sure did nice things for a man's body.

I forced my gaze back to his face and found his focus on me. One brow was cocked high as an amused smile tugged at one corner of his mouth.

It spread into a full out grin and I felt my face grow hot as blood flooded my cheeks.

Yeah, that wasn't too embarrassing! Getting caught staring at his pecs.

Needing an escape, I stood.

"Done?" I grabbed my empty dessert plate and then his, thinking the diversion of carrying them both to the sink was exactly what I needed.

There at least I could hide my red face for a moment.

Cash came up behind me as I stood facing the sink. He slid a plate next to me on the counter and said, "I believe this cookie is yours."

I hadn't counted on Cash getting up and carrying over the serving plate that contained the one remaining uneaten cookie. I swallowed hard and glanced down at the heart-shaped cookie that had *RED HOT* printed on it in big bold letters.

Thanks, Bethany, for that choice of sugary sayings.

What did this mean? Was Cash saying he thought I was hot? Me? Freckles and all?

He was standing so closely behind me that the scent of the fabric softener in his clothes reached my nose. Fabric softener had never smelled so sexy.

"Mine?" I asked, since my brain wasn't working right now as my heart pounded.

"Yeah. I had two cookies and you only ate one. So, this one is yours," he explained, deflating my balloon of hope with one sharp stab of reality.

"Oh. You can have it. I certainly don't need to eat any more sweets."

It was ridiculous, me facing the sink when I wasn't even washing the dishes. They were going to go in the dishwasher anyway. Time to turn around and face him.

I turned and saw the crooked smile that made me want to nibble on his lips.

"No," he said. "That cookie says *Red Hot*, so that one definitely belongs to you."

Maybe he was calling me hot after all.

But no. My name was Red. That had to be why.

Chastising myself for being silly once again, I forced out a short laugh. "Because of my name."

"Well yeah," he nodded. "But also, because you're hot."

I felt my eyes widen at his comment. I probably looked like a cartoon character with my eyes bulging out, which was the opposite of hot.

But holy moley, he'd said I was hot.

He had, hadn't he?

I felt for a second like I might have imagined the whole thing. As if I'd fantasized about this man and this moment so often, I couldn't tell reality from delusion anymore.

But then he leaned lower and I could see the tiny scar on his upper lip where he'd gotten cut during a particularly vicious snowball fight during recess in seventh grade.

And I could smell the coffee on his breath as his lips parted and he leaned closer, exhaling as his hazel eyes focused on me.

It felt like he was thinking about kissing me. Then he leaned in closer.

Holy crap. He *was* going to kiss me.

Cashel Morgan was leaning in for a kiss. Our first kiss. The kiss I'd wanted since I was a pre-teen. Only now, unlike then, a kiss would open up a whole world of possibilities between us.

I was an adult. He was an adult. I lived alone in an apartment with a nice private bedroom outfitted with a beautiful antique iron bed with an almost brand-new ergonomic mattress.

Just thinking about where this kiss could lead had me parting my lips as he reached out and wrapped his big strong hands around my upper arms.

My eyes drifted closed as I anticipated the first touch of his lips to mine . . . and then he cussed and dropped his hands from me.

My lids flew open just as he leaned away, then took a step back.

"I have to go."

"What? Why?" I squeaked.

What the heck? What had just happened here?

Flustered. Confused. I ran after him, baffled and, truth be told, kind of insulted as he strode for the door.

He was not just leaving, but leaving at a near sprint.

Having to grab his jacket from the hook next to the door slowed his exit enough I could catch up.

He glanced at me as he pulled his jacket on over his broad shoulders and thick arms and said one word. "Fire."

Fire?

Then I heard it and realized I'd been so engulfed

in my fantasies about kissing Cashel I hadn't even heard the fire whistle.

The firehouse was on the other side of town so in my defense I wasn't that oblivious. The sound was muted by distance and the massive amounts of insulation I'd installed when I'd renovated the top floor of the carriage house to be my home.

But Cash had heard it. As a volunteer, it was probably wired into him to be on alert.

Darn. Could I have worse luck or worse timing?

I could swear I saw regret coupled with longing in his gaze as he reached for the doorknob. "Thanks for dinner."

"Sure. You're welcome."

He took one step forward than glanced back. "See you later?"

Was that a question mark I heard at the end of that sentence? And did that mean that I would indeed see him later if I said yes?

"Yeah." I managed a breathy answer as Cash nodded, and then he was gone. But the schoolgirl who still lived inside me and the adult both looked forward to seeing him again. Very soon.

Two hours later there was a knock on my door.

I'd cleaned up everything from dinner and had just put on my pajamas to settle in for a night in front of the television when the sound startled me.

I rarely got anyone knocking on my door and never this late at night.

"Red, you up?" Cash's voice settled my nerves as

I'd been deciding if I should grab the cast iron frying pan in self-defense.

Cash was back.

When I made that wish—that I'd see Cash soon and we'd pick up where we left off—I had no idea it would be now.

My pulse raced as I struggled to extricate myself from the winter cocoon I was ensconced in on the sofa. My fleece pajama bottoms and the thick fur-lined throw acted like Velcro, trapping me in a tangled mess.

"Coming!" I called as I nearly fell on my face trying to stand while still a prisoner of my winter comfort.

Finally, I managed to stumble to the door while leaving the throw on the floor behind me.

Before I reached for the lock I hiked up the elastic band of my bottoms that had gotten tugged down to my hips from the struggle. It was about then that I realized exactly what I was wearing.

The last thing I wanted was for Cash to see me in my smiley face pajama bottoms.

Scratch that. The dead last thing I wanted was for Cash to leave before I got the door open because I'd taken so long. There was no way I was taking the time to change now.

I flipped the deadbolt and then the lock on the knob, finally yanking the door open with both hands.

His smile was as captivating as it was cocky as he took me in from the toes of my Grinch green socks, to the aforementioned yellow smiley face bottoms, to my old *Mudville 4-H* T-shirt.

"Nice outfit," he said.

"Yeah, thanks," I said, with as much sarcasm as I could muster.

My heart was vibrating my body, it was pounding so hard.

It didn't help that Cash began to look a bit unsure of himself as we both stood there in the doorway, barely a foot apart but with me on the inside and him on the outside.

The silence was deafening. It didn't help either of us, I was sure, so I decided to break it.

"How was the fire?" I asked. A ridiculous question, I knew, but I couldn't come up with any other topic at the moment.

He'd left his fire fighter overalls on and they were hella distracting.

Holy cow, did he look hot in his uniform. If Harper knew what she was doing she'd be writing fire fighter heroes for her romance books because damn, he looked good.

"Ended up not being a fire. Just a tree shooting sparks where it fell on a power line."

"Oh," I said. "That's good though. I mean not good it was on the power line, but good it wasn't a fire or anything worse."

He nodded, his hands braced on the doorframe as he hovered halfway between being inside and outside.

Finally, he said, "I forgot something when I was

here before."

"You did? What?" I asked, wondering if his cell phone had been in between my sofa cushions all this time and I could have been snooping in it.

I had no doubt his passcode would be something simple, like his birthdate, and I'd known that since kindergarten when his mom brought in cupcakes.

"This," Cash said as he stepped forward and pulled me into his arms.

This time he didn't hesitate. Didn't hover. His warm lips covered mine in a hot kiss that knocked me off balance and back a step.

I grabbed on to his jacket with both fists to make sure I didn't get any farther away if his kiss threw me further off balance.

He tipped his head, taking the kiss deeper as his tongue parted my lips. I happily allowed him access.

This kiss was everything. Everything I'd imagined. Everything I'd hoped for. Everything I'd been living without until now.

The one thing I knew for certain was that I didn't want to live without it again. Didn't want another moment that his lips weren't on mine.

Cash groaned. The sound cut through me, straight down to long neglected parts.

But then he pulled back from the kiss. He watched me through narrowed eyes as he drew in and blew out a big breath.

It was like the oxygen brought him back to his senses. He dropped his hold on me and took a step back, just when I wanted him to stay right where he was.

"All right." He nodded. "Good night."

What? He was leaving?

I took a step forward, so many things on the tip of my tongue. When would I see him again? And where did this leave us? Were we friends who kissed occasionally, such as when it was late at night and we'd had too many heart cookies? Or was this more?

As it ended up, I didn't say anything besides, "Okay. Good night."

He smiled as his gaze lingered on me for longer than necessary before he turned and left, leaving me confused.

There was one possible explanation for Cash's odd behavior tonight, but I was having trouble wrapping my head around it.

Was Cashel Morgan a gentleman?

That might be the biggest surprise of all. And the most irresistible.

CHAPTER ELEVEN

Cash

"So, Cash, you got home late last night." Stone's comment dripped with suggestion.

It wasn't a shock to me he was acting like a smart ass.

What was a shock was that Stone was actually at the farm at the right time to help unload the feed.

Stone being home was a rarity nowadays since he spent so much of his time with Harper at Agnes's place. I should be happy he was around to help with the chores. I was not happy he was around to pry into my business.

"Yup." I cocked a brow and shot him a sideways glance, answering the question he hadn't actually asked with one word, which was all he deserved.

"Hot night, I guess. Huh?" Stone continued.

"Yup." I smiled and decided to play with him a bit. "Downright explosive."

I shot Boone a glance. My little brother chuckled,

quick to pick up on what I was up to. Boone could be dense sometimes, but when it came to sibling sparring, he was always right on the ball.

Taunting Stone was one of my favorite things to do.

It was especially fun today because he had already convinced himself that I strolled in late last night because I'd been getting busy with Red, when in fact, the lateness of the hour had nothing to do with my dinner and everything to do with the damn tree that had fallen on the power lines.

I was confident in this plan to lead Stone into a false sense of superiority and then knock him down because Boone had been at the call with me.

Of course, I'd gotten the expected inquisition from Boone last night, but since it had been early, he believed me when I'd told him I'd just barely finished eating when the whistle blew.

Since Boone and I were the two who routinely got yanked out of our warm beds, and away from our hot dates, because of our service to the community, and Stone for reasons of his own that I couldn't comprehend did not volunteer, I figured he was fair game for taunting.

Of course, I had made that one very short but oh so eventful detour to Red's place on the way home from the fire call, but Boone didn't know about that so it didn't count.

I'd told him I was stopping to gas up the truck and I'd see him at home. And I had filled up the truck— earlier that day—but the stop at Red's took about the same amount of time, so I figured I was in the clear.

Meanwhile, Stone was still looking cocky. Like he had something on me. Which he most certainly did not.

"So, is there going to be a repeat?" Stone asked, as I wondered when he'd become such an old wash woman.

"I hope not," Boone said. "I'm not sure that tree can take a repeat of last night."

I burst out in a laugh. "True that."

Stone frowned. "What are you talking about? What tree?"

I waited to allow Boone to explain, figuring the story would hold more credibility if it came from him.

"We got called to a fire last night. Tree leaning on the power lines shooting sparks everywhere. Lucky it didn't blow the transformer. But that's where we were from just before eight until about ten last night. Cash was with me and the fire crew. Not with Red."

Stone glared at me. "Why didn't you just say that?"

"What fun would that be?" I grinned. "Besides, if you did your civic duty like the two of us and joined the fire department you would have known where I was and what I was doing."

He scowled, but at least it shut him up for the time being.

After a smile at Boone I went back to doing what I'd come to the barn to do, unload and stack the bags of feed in the back of Boone's truck.

The truth was, hell yes, I would like a repeat of

that kiss last night with Red, but there was no way I would tell either of my brothers that or the details of my dinner with her—intimate or other.

However, that didn't mean I couldn't pry into their private lives.

I knew Boone had been in the middle of a heated game of pool at the bar when the call had come in. He'd had to forfeit and that had caused him to go on a nice long rant while we diverted traffic and waited for the power company to come.

But Stone was still ripe to be plucked.

"So, what were *you* so busy doing last night when the whistle blew that you didn't even hear it, big brother?" I asked him.

I hadn't noticed his truck parked at Agnes's when I'd driven by. Which was odd.

He rolled his eyes. "I didn't hear it because I was in Vestal."

"Vestal? Why?" I frowned.

"Harper misses *real* shopping at *real* stores, as she put it. Apparently, she'll buy everything, including chicken feed, online but when it comes to certain things, she wants to go to a store to get it. And the nearest store she wanted to go to happens to be in Vestal."

Boone laughed. "Sorry, bro. But if you wanna play, you gotta pay."

I had to agree with Boone. Stone got a lot of perks from Harper for a pretty small price, in my opinion.

An occasional trip to Vestal in exchange for all the

times he rolled in after midnight after being with her—yeah, he was getting away cheap as far as I could see.

"What did she buy?" Boone asked.

The kid was freakily into minute details. Even if I had been mildly curious about what purchase had inspired Harper to drag Stone to Vestal, I hadn't bothered asking about it.

"Pajama bottoms." Stone scowled.

Bursting out with a laugh, I had to admit I was suitably amused that Stone had driven almost an hour each way for pajama bottoms, until the memory of Red looking adorable in her smiley face bottoms drained all the blood away from my brain.

"Were they nice ones?" Boone asked, which only had Stone scowling deeper and me laughing harder.

What made the moment even more precious was when Harper, the pajama queen herself, walked in. Or actually, ran in and skidded to a stop.

Stone may bitch a bit, but one look at his girl's distraught face had him dropping the bag of feed back into the truck bed, jumping down to the ground and striding to her. "What's wrong?"

She was breathing heavily and looked close to tears. It was enough that I dropped the bag in my hands on the pile and strode over too.

Stone grabbed her shoulders and leaned low to say, "Harper, tell me."

"It's . . ." She paused to let out a big breath. "It's so horrible. People are so horrible. This town, I swear."

Harper was a master storyteller. Like literally. She was a professional, award winning, bestselling writer, but whatever had happened today had been so upsetting, Stone couldn't get a straight answer out of her.

"What are you talking about?" he asked. "Start from the beginning. Slow."

As Boone wandered closer to stand next to me, she sucked in a gulp of air. Finally, she said, "Last night, Red found a cow."

"Wait, what?" Now she had my attention. I took a step closer. "Red found a *cow*? Last night?"

She nodded but I still didn't know what she was talking about.

I was five seconds away from pulling out my cell to call Red and get the whole story when she finally pulled herself together enough to calm down and start explaining.

"A baby cow must have escaped from the stock auction and was in Bethany's yard. She didn't know what to do so she texted Red. So of course, Red went over to help her."

Of course, she did. I could picture it now. Red and Bethany chasing after a calf. Baby or not, that calf wasn't going to want to be caught.

My lips twitched at the vision in my brain. I'd pay good money to see a video of how that went down.

"So, Red caught it," Harper continued.

"Caught it how?" Boone asked.

116

"Bethany said Red had a cookie as bait and a dog leash from the store to tie it up. She like jumped on it, got the leash around its neck and somehow was able to get it back to her carriage house. And that's when she posted a picture of it on Facebook. Because, you know, it was cute."

Of course, she'd post it on Facebook, because that's what Red did.

I smiled again, about to take out my cell to find this picture when Harper said, "Then the nastiness started. And the threats. And all the mean people in this town showed their true colors."

My smile faded. "What do you mean?"

"There are all sorts of nasty comments on her Facebook post. Then some people started private messaging her. Saying she stole that cow because it belongs to the auction house. Someone said they were going to turn her in and she'd go to jail. Then other mean people were sending her pictures of steaks and telling her he was going to be veal chops soon once the auction house got him back."

Harper leaned into Stone as he rubbed her back, comforting her.

Meanwhile, I needed a little comforting myself because I was getting pissed off. How could people be such dicks to Red for trying to help a helpless animal?

"She didn't steal it. The auction was days ago. It must have been running loose all this time," Boone pointed out the obvious.

"Well, whether they had a case against her or not,

they really upset her. She was crying when she called me. She's worried if she doesn't return it—which of course she doesn't want to because, you know, veal—then they could say she did steal it. She said she was contacting the authorities to see what she could work out."

"What authorities?" I asked, realizing now was not the time to be jealous she might have called Carson, but I had to ask anyway.

"I don't know. But she was going to call the owner of the stock auction too, to try to buy the cow. She's really upset by this. I don't blame her. He's so cute with those big brown puppy dog eyes, I don't think she can part with him now. She sat up with him all night in the little pen she built in her carriage house."

I could picture that. But at the same time, I was disappointed that she didn't feel she could call me for help. Instead, she'd obviously called Harper instead.

"What do you think's going to happen?" She turned her teary eyes to Stone.

He cringed. "Harper, you have to understand that small farmers make a living raising and selling cattle for meat."

"I know that. And I'm not a complete hypocrite. I eat meat and wear leather. What I'm saying is this poor baby cow was running around town for days, starving, probably dehydrated, cold, scared, and no one bothered to report it or look for it? Then, now that Red found it, people say it's not hers and she has to give it back? How is that right? Isn't there such a thing as finders keepers?"

Stone was obviously between a rock and a hard place, no pun intended. Agree with his girl, or his hard place would not be rocking into her any time soon.

Personally, I could see Harper's side. This calf had been basically abandoned by the auction company— probably already written off as a loss. A cost of doing business. And Red had gone to the trouble of capturing it and caring for it.

But on the other hand, Stone was right in that this calf was not a pet. It had originated as a valuable asset to a small farmer who'd brought it to auction to sell to put food on the table for his family.

And what the hell did Red think she was going to do with it when it was no longer such an adorable little *baby cow*, as my brother's city-born girlfriend kept calling it?

More than that, Harper kept calling it a *he*. If this calf was indeed a male, which it might well be if it had been in the meat pen for sale, it would soon become a bull. And bulls did not make the best of pets.

Harper's Aunt Agnes might have successfully rescued and made a pet out of that pig of hers that had escaped from the auction, but not all escaped livestock could be domesticated.

The future of the calf aside, I was most worried about Red and how this was affecting her.

I knew the woman. I'd bet better than she thought I did. I'd personally seen customers treat her with a complete lack of common courtesy, and she'd respond with a smile and a kind word. Not only did her business depend on it, but I think that was just the kind of person she was. The type to show kindness in the face of those being far from kind.

But how long before they broke her? Before she couldn't take any more? I would have cracked long ago.

Boone cringed. "It's only a matter of time before the town slaps a violation on her. Fining people is Animal Control's favorite pastime."

"Boone's right. There are rules about keeping animals in the village." Stone nodded.

"What about Petunia?" Harper asked.

Stone shook his head. "Agnes only gets away with having Petunia because the board voted in a special variance just for her."

Boone nodded. "Yeah, and they only got away with doing that by making Petunia the official Mudville Hogs mascot."

"Well we need to do something. We need to help Red," Harper said.

I agreed whole heartedly with Harper. Red hadn't asked for my help, but I was going to help her anyway. Somehow.

"How?" Stone asked, looking at a loss.

"I don't know. Can't Morgan Farm buy the cow, legally, so they can't take it back to the auction?" Harper asked.

Stone shrugged. "I mean, I guess. If they're willing to sell it. And at a fair price."

I scowled at my frugal older brother. "I don't care

if it's a fair price or not. I'll pay for it out of my own damn pocket if I have to."

Stone shot me a glance and finally sighed. "All right. I'll call the guy at the auction and see what I can do."

I had the number for the office of the guy who ran the auction in my phone too, but since I was a wee bit emotionally involved in this because of Red, I let Stone make the call.

As the older Morgan brother, and probably the heir apparent to the family business in the eyes of the auction company, he was the best choice anyway. And if there was one thing Stone did do well, it was act like he was the boss around here. For once, that would come in handy.

I'd never realized how annoying it was to only hear one side of a phone conversation until now. Between Stone's *yups* and *nopes* and the occasional *I see* and *I understand*, I was ready to wrestle the cell out of his hand and take over myself.

Finally, he disconnected the call and glanced around at all of us. I didn't like the expression on his face or the way he was dragging his feet to report what had been said.

Apparently, neither did Harper. "What's happening?" she demanded.

"Red is there right now at the office," Stone said.

"That's good, right? She must be there to pay for the calf," Boone guessed.

Stone drew in a breath. "No. Not exactly. The sheriff's department and somebody from Animal

Control are both there too, to supervise the calf being turned over to the rightful owner. The auction house."

"What?" Harper's eyes widened as my own narrowed.

Stone nodded. My only solace was that he didn't look happy as he said, "They were just about to head over to Red's to get it."

Fucking idiots.

Couldn't they see how much this calf meant to this woman? And they couldn't see clear to selling it to her, or to us even?

There was only way to deal with idiots. You couldn't argue with them, but you could go around them. And that's exactly what I was going to do.

Turning on my heel, I stalked out of the barn, past Boone's truck and directly toward my own.

"Where are you going?"

I heard Boone's question behind me but I didn't respond.

First of all, there was no time to waste. Second, though Boone and Harper would support me, I was pretty sure Stone wouldn't like my answer.

I might have sped a little bit getting to Red's place, but I adhered to the speed limit coming back home.

First off, I really didn't want to get pulled over with a stolen calf, hog tied and hidden under a blanket, in the bed of my official Morgan Farm pick-up truck. And second, I was transporting precious cargo. The calf Red had fallen in love with.

This might be the one thing in the world that I could give Red that no other man could. The life of this, admittedly, exceptionally cute little calf.

The calf who was, without doubt, a girl, not a boy. Thank goodness for that. It not turning out to be a bull would definitely help when it came time to admit to my parents what I'd done. And when it came time to assimilate this little girl in with our own milk herd.

I had to plan ahead for that even though, up until now, planning ahead was something I didn't generally do.

Funny how I was looking to the future now . . . and not just in regard to this calf.

CHAPTER TWELVE

Red

I stared at the owner of the stock company in disbelief.

In fact, I'd been walking around pretty much in a constant state of disbelief ever since Bethany's text last night just before midnight.

Silly me had thought it might be a booty text from Cash, and I'd been open to it. Then I'd seen it was from Bethany about a stray calf running around her yard.

Things had just gotten crazier from there.

The calf. The evil people in town threatening me. And now this—the owner of the stock auction going back on his word to sell me the calf.

I tried to keep my cool as I said, "Mr. Philbin, you said on the phone that I could buy the calf for fair market value."

That was why I had closed up the shop, driven to the office and was standing there with my checkbook in my hand trying to pay the man for the calf currently stashed in my carriage house.

"Did I?" The man lifted one shoulder.

I felt my blood pressure rise. Torn between anger and tears, I only hoped I could keep from breaking down in front of this bastard. He didn't deserve to think he had the power to make me cry.

The door behind me opened, making his focus move from me to whoever had come in. I turned to see who that was and frowned as Carson Bekker, in uniform, walked in.

"What are you doing here?" I asked.

"Got a call at the department asking for somebody to come over here. Something about having to recover some livestock. I was told it might possibly be a hostile situation."

Hostile situation.

I felt my nostrils flare as my jaw clenched. "Is that what they said?" I turned slowly and glared at the older man through narrowed eyes before turning back to Carson. "Well, I hope you brought backup. You know, in case you can't control me and all my hostility."

"This is about you?" Carson asked, a furrow forming between his eyes.

"Apparently." I cocked a brow high.

Carson's appearance and the information he'd revealed had worked to move me further away from tears and smack into the middle of the anger zone.

"This woman is holding one of my calves at her place," Philbin said, looking as if he believed he was firmly on the side of right. We were in a gray area as far as I was concerned.

Carson's brows drew lower. "Where are you keeping a calf at your place?"

There was one good thing. If anyone would listen to my side of the story, it would be Carson.

"For now, the carriage house," I answered. "But now that you're here, maybe you can help."

Carson nodded. "I'll do my best. If somebody tells me what's going on."

"I—" Philbin began.

"*I'll* tell this story," I said, shooting a glare at him before looking back to Carson. "A calf escaped during the last auction. The poor thing was on the loose for days when it wandered into Bethany's yard. It was cold and hungry and thirsty and as far as I can tell no one was looking for it and, correct me if I'm wrong, no one had reported it. So, I took it to my place then contacted the office here to offer to buy it."

Even though the bastards hadn't even been looking for the poor thing.

Carson nodded. "All right. So why am I here to go get the calf?"

"Mr. Philbin said I could buy it on the phone for fair market value, but now he's reneging."

Looking very official with his hands resting casually on his gun belt, Carson asked, "What's the problem, Mr. Philbin? Why did you change your mind about selling Miss Meyer the animal?"

"I don't need a reason. The animal belongs to me. I don't have to sell it if I don't want to."

"See, that's where we disagree. Does the animal belong to him? Isn't possession nine-tenths of the law?" I asked Carson.

"Look, I can prove it's mine. It's got my tag in its ear. I've got all the paperwork," Philbin continued, indicating the stack of papers on the very messy desk.

Carson drew in a breath and cut his gaze to me. "He's got proof the calf is his property, Red."

"But he wasn't even looking for it," I defended, resisting the urge to stamp my foot in frustration. "The poor thing could have starved or frozen to death and he didn't lift a finger to try and find it."

While we talked, or rather while I tried to sway Carson to my way of thinking, Philbin stepped out of the room to take a phone call.

Carson looked pained, torn between doing what the law said he had to and what he really wanted to. "I know, Red. And believe me I'm going to put all that in the report. We can levy a fine on him for not reporting the animal missing. There are proper procedures that have to be followed when livestock gets loose in the village. But there's also no question that the animal is his property."

They kept calling the calf *property,* but over the hours I'd been with her, she'd become more than an animal, more than a commodity to me. I'd fallen in love with her as her big brown eyes looked up at me while I bottle fed her milk.

And yes, I was very aware I'd had a big juicy steak

for dinner just hours before I'd rescued the calf. But I'd gotten to know her over the night and this morning.

She had a personality. She recognized me when I walked in the carriage house. I swear she knew I'd saved her and was grateful.

Just like Petunia over at Agnes's place, this little girl felt more like a pet than a product to be sold.

She'd been so hungry. So scared. I'd fed her. I'd made her a bed and set up a heater so she'd be warm. I'd sat with her for hours to make sure she was all right. She should be mine, free and clear. Not the stock company's.

I firmly believed that, but even so, I was willing to pay the man for her. And now he wouldn't let me, in spite of what he'd said on the phone.

What kind of person did that? Broke their word? Backed out of an oral contract?

A horrible one, that's what kind.

Just as horrible as all those mean people commenting on my Facebook post. And the one who'd called me on the phone in the shop to tell me off. And the other one who'd come into the store to yell at me. They seemed to be willing to go out of their way to accuse me of being a stock thief or taunt me about how the calf would make some nice veal chops.

People were terrible.

But no, not all people. For every one mean spirited person, there were ten who felt the same as I did. Who commended me on giving the calf a safe and warm place to stay. Who felt she'd earned the right to live a long happy life when she escaped from the stock auction and survived days and nights on the loose all on her own.

The door opened again, triggering the door alert. Philbin returned to the room, still on his phone as a man in another Mudville uniform walked in.

"Now who is this?" I mumbled, mostly to myself.

"Animal control." Carson cringed as he glanced at me. "I called them. I didn't know what I was walking into and I thought I might need help recovering the livestock."

I cocked a brow high. "It's a baby calf. I picked it up by myself and put it in the truck last night."

"Again, I didn't know that. I had no idea what I was walking into here."

I sighed. "I know."

This wasn't Carson's fault. And since he was my only ally, I should probably be nicer to him.

But I was all out of nice at the moment. It had been beaten out of me by Mr. Philbin and the mean people of Mudville.

"We ready?" the animal control officer asked Carson just as Mr. Philbin disconnected his call and stashed the cell in his jacket pocket.

"I sure as hell am," Philbin said, stepping around the desk.

Carson glanced at me and then nodded to the animal control guy. "Yeah. Follow me over."

I followed the group out and got into my truck

and that's when it hit me. They were taking her. And I knew what would happen to her next.

The tears blurred my vision as I followed the line of vehicles toward Main Street, led slowly by Carson. The whole thing had the feel of a funeral procession to it. In a way, that's kind of what it was.

It wasn't far, but I wished it had been. Every mile brought me closer to the time I'd have to say goodbye to my little girl. I'd be doing it with tears in my eyes and I was sure that bastard Philbin would notice and probably take great joy in the fact he'd broken my spirit. And at this point there was no denying it was good and broken.

Then what? Once they'd taken her and left, what would I do with myself?

The dead last thing I wanted to do was go back to that shop, stand behind the cash register and smile. I just didn't have it in me. I was done. At least for today.

If Gretchen couldn't come in to cover, I'd just stay closed for the day. I'd incur the wrath of the shoppers who just didn't get that a solo entrepreneur needed a day off sometimes. And I'd lose a day's worth of sales. But I didn't have a choice. If one more person said something to me about that calf, I was going to lose it.

The whole situation was too much. How could I watch them pick her up and toss her in the back of the Animal Control van? But how could I not be there for her?

As Carson pulled up in front of my place, I knew it

was going to take me a long time to get over this. If I
ever did.

Carson paused, waiting for me to park in the
driveway and get out of the truck.

"Ready?" he asked.

"No," I said honestly.

He reached out like he was going to touch my
shoulder, then dropped his hand, as if he thought
better of it.

At least he didn't take joy in this, unlike that rotten
Philbin.

The Animal Control van pulled up next to us.
"Where is it?"

It. Like she wasn't even a living animal. I opened
my mouth to answer but didn't know if I'd get the
words out. Instead, I pointed toward the carriage
house.

Carson, watching me, answered, "The calf's in
there."

The guy frowned. "You know, you can't keep
livestock in the village."

"I know. It was only temporary," I said, annoyed
even in my distressed state.

"You wanna let us in?" Carson asked, watching
me.

"No, but I suppose I will so you don't arrest me."

Carson pressed his lips together and drew in a
breath but didn't reply.

When all this was over—long, long over—I was

going to owe him an apology.

Until then, I stomped to the door. I gripped the handle and tugged, sliding the big wooden door along the metal rail and exposing my makeshift pen.

"She's in there," I said, not looking yet as I braced myself to face my little girl after I'd failed her.

"Where?" Carson asked.

"Right th—" I stopped mid word as I turned and saw the pen was empty. "What the heck?"

I stepped inside and looked around the piles of clutter I'd had to move to make room for the pen. There was barely room to walk, forget about space for a calf to hide, no matter how small. But maybe, with as frightened as she was, she'd wedged herself behind something.

"What are you trying to pull here?" Philbin asked, the accusation clear in his tone.

"I'm not trying to pull anything." I spun toward him, hands on my hips.

"You're saying it just escaped?" he spat, looking doubtful.

"Since this calf escaped from you just four days ago and you're the expert stock handler running a supposedly professional operation, what makes it so inconceivable that she could escape from my carriage house? Huh?"

Carson, playing the sleuth, had his flashlight out and was searching the area.

"The back door is ajar," he said, before moving back to the pen I'd created. "And this barricade has a couple of gaps big enough I imagine a small calf could have squeezed out."

"That means she's out there again on the loose." Worse, I'd heard it was supposed to be bitter cold tonight.

"So, you're not going to arrest her?" Philbin asked Carson.

I'd been so worried about the once again missing calf, I hadn't realized I needed to be worried for myself. I shot a concerned glance at Carson and wondered if I had enough money in the bank to pay Dee Flanders and make bail if I ended up in jail and needed a lawyer.

"No, sir. I'm not," Carson said, allaying my fear.

Philbin sighed. "I'm heading back to the office."

"Aren't you going to search for her?" I asked him.

"No, Miss Meyer. I've wasted enough time on this already. I think I'll let you search, since you have so much experience in livestock search and rescue. You let me know when you find it. Then I'll send somebody over to pick it up." The son of a bitch even had the nerve to grin at me before he turned to walk away.

Over my dead body would I let him know if I found that calf again. This time I'd drive her over state lines if I had to, just to keep her away from this miserly man.

But none of that would be a concern if I couldn't find her. Carson came back to me after speaking to the Animal Control officer. He stood next to me and stared at the empty pen.

"What if I can't find her again?" I asked.

"We're on Main Street. Somebody'll spot her." He turned to face me. "And if they report it, I'll give you a call. Okay?"

"You'd do that for me? Even after the way I've treated you today?" I asked.

"Of course. I know you're upset and you have every right to be. That guy is a dick. You know I'm on your side, right? But at the same time, I do have to do my job."

"I know." I had to admit, Carson was a really good guy.

He'd make some girl a great boyfriend. Too bad I was so hung up on Cash, that girl couldn't be me.

"Oh, and I don't have anything new for you on the stuff you found in the attic over on Second Street."

Jeez. That whole thing with the missing—and then found—cape felt like a lifetime ago. "Thanks for the update."

"No problem." He looked like he was about to go and then hesitated. "One more thing."

"Yeah?"

"I just want you to know the only reason I haven't asked you out again is because I'm pretty sure you've got a thing for Cash."

Shocked, I opened my mouth, thinking I should deny it but not sure I could.

Carson held up a hand to silence my protest. "But, if it turns out I'm wrong about that and you wanna get together some night, you have my number."

He didn't wait for an answer. Instead he spun and walked toward his vehicle parked along the curb.

As he paused with the door open, he called back, "Good luck finding your calf."

Carson had just driven away and I hadn't even had time to come up with a plan for my new search yet when Harper's car skidded to a stop in the driveway.

She was out of the driver's seat and to me in seconds.

"What's happening? You didn't answer my texts. And Bethany hadn't heard from you either." Her gaze cut to the empty pen. "Uh oh. Where's the cow?"

I blew out a breath. "I wish I knew."

CHAPTER THIRTEEN

Cash

"Where have you been?" Stone asked.

"Nowhere," I said as I moved to grab a bale of hay to toss to the horses for their afternoon feeding.

Stone crossed his arms over his chest and watched me. "First you run out of here without a word, then you disappear for well over an hour. And now you say you've been nowhere."

"I'm not saying I agree with your summary of my afternoon, but all right, let's say I do. What's your point?" I asked.

Annoyed, as I'd hoped, Stone let out a huff. "My point is, you had to be some place."

Actually, I'd been many places. Red's carriage house, where I'd nabbed the calf. The old shed on the back of our property here, where I'd stashed the calf.

My secret errand took longer than I'd hoped it would and I'd been missed.

The calf was young, so I'd had to feed it with a bottle and set it up with enough straw it could stay warm until I could slip it in with our calves. But I couldn't do that until I had time to remove the auction house's ear tag. That was evidence I wanted gone.

Stone didn't need to know any of that.

"Nope. I wasn't anywhere." I shook my head, then pinned Stone with a stare. "Shouldn't you be with your girl? She seemed pretty upset last I saw her."

"Harper went over to Red's. She figured Red would need the support after they came and took back the calf."

"Hmm. Good idea." I nodded.

It was all I could do to control my grin knowing that the auction company wasn't getting that calf back. Not today. Not while I was around to prevent it.

Of course, Red wouldn't know I had the animal. I'd left the back door open so they'd think it could have gotten out on its own and not blame her.

Did they believe that? Did Red? What was she thinking right now?

It could be pretty much anything. And she could be just as upset as if they had taken the calf from her. At that sobering thought I no longer had trouble controlling my grin.

I needed to finish these chores and get over to her place.

138

Whether I was going to tell her the truth or not was still up in the air in my mind. I wanted her to have plausible deniability.

If she didn't know what had happened, she couldn't be blamed for it. If I got caught, I wanted it to fall on me, not her.

God willing, I wouldn't get caught. My father would flip. And Morgan Farm didn't need that kind of negative press.

Even if all I did was provide more suitable accommodations for my friend's calf that she'd found roaming the streets of Mudville, I was probably technically breaking the law.

If the stock company found out what I'd done and decided to come after me, I could get in a lot of trouble. Red hadn't stolen the calf the way folks had accused her of doing, but by moving it out of her place, I suppose they could say I had stolen it.

I'd been raised that only bad people stole. Funny, I didn't feel like a bad guy.

Not after hearing from Harper about how mean people were being to Red and seeing it for myself on her Facebook post. Then, hearing how the auction owner wouldn't even accept our money to buy the calf fair and square—it had all forced my hand.

Had everyone acted like decent human beings from the beginning, that calf would be bought and paid for and happily living with the Morgan calves. But, as it turned out, there were a few real nasty apples spoiling the Mudville barrel.

Hell, I guess I could always throw some cash in an envelope and shove it under the auction company's door. That way I could walk away with a clear conscience and they wouldn't be out the small amount the tiny thing would have gotten them at the sale.

But I still had to figure out what to do about Red.

How could I ease her mind about the calf without tipping my hand? That one would be a lot harder to accomplish than paying back the stock company.

Stone was still there staring at me as I pondered my next course of action. I had to get him off my case. Then I had to get the horses fed so I could get the hell out of here and over to Red's place to see what state she was in.

"You going to stand there like the King of England watching me? Or you gonna help?" I asked, figuring that would accomplish both tasks.

Stone scowled, grumbling something about kings and queens I didn't have much interest in listening to. But he did walk over and start filling the feed buckets while I threw more hay into the stalls.

Mission accomplished. At least the two most immediately pressing issues had been handled. Stone was busy and no longer talking and the horses were being fed.

Hopefully the rest of my issues would be resolved as easily and smoothly.

Red was in the store when I walked in the door about an hour later. Gretchen was behind the register but the customer standing at the counter wasn't there to buy anything from what I could see.

It looked like she was there to yell at Red. And though Red stood silently and took the dressing down, I could see she was seething inside. Her cheeks were flushed. Her breathing short and rapid.

She looked about as stressed as I feared she would. But I'd been assuming she'd be upset after finding the calf missing. Not from getting more abuse from the less than fine citizens of Mudville. And abuse was the best word I could come up with given the incredibly cruel things the woman was saying to Red.

"I bet you stole that calf and let it loose just so you could post about it on Facebook. That's what this reward you set up is really about. Not the calf. It's all to get publicity for your shop, you . . . you . . . social media whore," the horrible woman spat.

The word *whore* pushed me over the edge as much as the ridiculous accusation.

"All right. That's enough." I stepped forward and grabbed Red's arm, taking only enough time to get a good look at the face of the woman who would be going on my shit list before I steered Red away and into the office.

I didn't stop there and reached for the knob on the back door. I glanced at her before opening it.

"Your girl okay here alone if we leave?"

She nodded. The color in her cheeks had started to fade, leaving her pale and looking shell shocked.

It was more than time to get the fuck out of this place. I opened the door and pulled her through and outside with me.

I was well versed with Red's carriage house after the last couple of days. I got us inside and closed the door, before bringing her over to the staircase and setting her up on the bottom step. That put her eye level with me so I could really get a good look at her and assess what level of damage I'd have to fix after she'd been emotionally attacked.

I was still fuming at how she'd been treated, feeling protective of this woman who didn't deserve any of the bull shit that had been thrown at her.

"You okay?" I asked, gripping her forearms, not willing to let her go.

She responded with a move that was half nod, half head shake, which gave me enough of an answer to know she was not okay.

I let out a sigh, wishing I could fix this with one well aimed punch at the offending party. Unfortunately, from what I'd seen, heard and read, there were a lot of assholes who had hurt her. And half of them were women. I couldn't solve this one with my fists.

She drew in a stuttering breath. "How can people be so mean about the reward? All I want to do is find her."

"What reward?" I asked.

I'd been confused about what the bitchy woman had been referring to, but it hadn't been the time to stop and ask questions.

"I posted on Facebook that I'd give a cash reward of two hundred dollars to anyone who caught the calf. I was only trying to make sure she was found. It's so cold and she's out there hungry and probably scared." Her voice broke on the last word as the tears started to flow.

"Shh. It's okay." I pulled her closer to me, trying to calm her fears without telling her the truth.

"No. It's not okay. I should have built a better pen. I should have made sure the back door was locked. It's my fault—"

"Red—"

"If she dies, it's because of me." She talked over me, her voice shaking as she did. "It's going to be below zero tonight—"

"Red. Stop. I have her." I pulled back far enough to see her face at my revelation.

In the waning light of late afternoon coming in the window on the staircase, I saw her frown. "What?"

The cat was out of the bag now. Might as well admit the truth. "I heard they were coming to take her away so I made sure I got here first." I lifted a shoulder.

Her eyes widened as she gripped my shoulders. "You have her?"

"Yes." I nodded.

"She's safe?"

"Yes."

"At your farm?"

"Yes."

For the first time today, her face brightened . . . then I couldn't see her face anymore as she pulled me to her and crashed her lips into mine.

It wasn't the reaction I'd expected, but I wasn't going to complain. Oh no. Instead, I kissed her back, wrapping her in my arms and enjoying my reward for playing the hero.

The kiss quickly went from gratitude to something much more. It wasn't long before I realized we needed to move to someplace a little more private.

With my tongue in her mouth and the hard-on from hell straining to get out of my jeans, I considered how I hadn't locked the carriage house door behind us.

Even knowing I had to stop, I couldn't help myself as I ran my hands down her body, pressing her closer against me and enjoying the pressure of her body against mine as I did.

I groaned as I forced myself to break the kiss, if not the embrace. I liked her against me, even if it would look pretty bad if someone walked in and caught us.

"We shouldn't do this here." But damn, I really wanted to do more of this.

She audibly swallowed and nodded, looking about as dazed as I felt. Her gaze met mine. "You really came and got her? For me?"

I let out a short laugh. "Of course. I'd do anything for you."

"Come upstairs." Her voice was husky, her cheeks flushed, her eyes narrowed.

The way she looked and the way I felt, for better or worse, she didn't have to ask me twice.

CHAPTER FOURTEEN

Red

I grabbed Cash's hand, marveling at how big and strong it felt in my smaller one.

Pulling him up the rickety wooden stairs, one hand on him, the other on the railing, I couldn't get into my apartment fast enough.

I managed to get the door open, but he's the one who closed and locked it behind us. Then he stood there, his green and gold-flecked hazel eyes focused intently on mine. In those eternally long few seconds I feared he'd change his mind. That he would leave.

But I didn't worry for long.

Gripping my face between his palms, he leaned down and pressed his lips to mine.

He kissed me, deep and enthusiastically. His tongue breached my lips and rubbed against mine in a motion that simulated what I'd like another part of him to be doing to a part of me.

One muscular leg nestled between mine. Shamelessly I enjoyed the friction it caused at the juncture between my thighs.

We might as well have been in high school again, making out while standing up, dry humping fully clothed. But with one huge difference. In high school Cash and I never did anything like this together.

Another difference—back in high school I had yet to experience my first orgasm. But I had a definite feeling I was about to have a doozy of one now.

My breath came fast and hard, but breathing wasn't easy since Cash continued to completely occupy my mouth.

When my thighs tightened around his and I started to shake and ride his leg like a pony, he pulled back and met my gaze.

Breathless himself, he asked, "Are you—"

"Yes," I gasped.

"Fuck," he breathed, his eyes narrowed with need.

He kissed me again, until the spasms had passed. Until blindly, I reached between us and started working on unfastening his belt buckle.

His throat worked as he swallowed. "Are you sure about this?"

"Yes . . ." I'd never been surer of wanting something in my life. "Why? Aren't you? Don't you want to—"

Cash let out a breath tinged with a short laugh. "Fuck yeah, I want to."

He blew out a breath and stared at the ceiling for a second before focusing back on me.

His hands covering mine at his waist, he said, "I'm trying to be a gentleman here, Red. But you're making that real hard."

"Well, stop trying. And for God's sake, for once stop talking." There was something hard between us and I wanted it.

I dropped to my knees, pushed his hands aside and finished the task of opening his jeans myself.

I freed him from his briefs and engulfed him between my lips. His mouth opened on a gasp and his eyes closed. He plunged the fingers of both hands into my hair and held my head still.

"I'm not gonna be able to hold on with you doing that."

"Then don't." I'd pulled off his length just long enough to say what I wanted, but I was already back to my task.

I must have been doing a good job at it too. Cash's breathing got more intense with every stroke of my hand and mouth over his cock. So did his cussing, intermingled with my name as he thrust into my mouth.

"Red, stop. I'm gonna come." He moved to pull out of my mouth but I gripped his ass and held him right there, swallowing down every drop that pulsed into my throat.

Still panting, Cash pulled me to my feet then pressed my head to his chest, wrapping both arms around me tight.

"Jesus, Red. You didn't have to do that."

149

I felt as much as heard the words vibrate through my ear. "I know I didn't have to. I wanted to," I replied, pulling back far enough I could see his face.

He glanced down at me. "I don't want you to feel like you owe me anything just because I hid that calf for you."

"I don't." I shook my head.

Did he not see that I'd been half in love with him since middle school? Were men really that blind? Were they all idiots?

Cash let out a breath. "I hate to say this, but I should go."

Go? I guess I had my answer. Idiots. Most likely every one of them, but certainly this one.

Taking a step back from Cash, I said, "Okay."

What was I going to do? Question him? Argue?

I wasn't in the position to do either. We were just casual friends . . . who'd recently happened to have seen each other orgasm.

He had asked me if I was sure. And I'd said yes. I couldn't blame anyone but myself.

He was simply acting like typical Cash. Here one moment, gone the next. Swooping in and back out again just as quickly, just like he did at my shop so often.

I turned to unlock the door for him, swinging it wide.

He stood a second in the doorway. "So, uh . . . thanks."

I let out a short laugh. "You're welcome."

He met my eyes then turned and trotted down the stairs.

Thanks?

In all the many, many times I'd imagined being with Cash, I'd never pictured it ending like this.

CHAPTER FIFTEEN
Cash

Minutes after saying goodbye to Red after our mind-boggling encounter in her apartment, I pulled into the driveway at home. Still feeling her mouth on me. Half hard again from the memory alone.

I'd left because people shouldn't see me spending hours with her since I was hiding her calf. I'd left because I needed to get home and feed that calf. But I'd mostly left because I was completely confused.

We had a good friendship, Red and I. One I valued. And I'd just fucking come in my friend's mouth.

There was no doubt I wanted her. And definitely no doubt I really didn't want her dating Carson or anybody else for that matter.

Where did we go from here?

Backwards would be more than awkward. Forward seemed frightening as hell.

Yup. Confusing as hell.

And now, I had to sneak out to the old shed on the other side of the property to feed the calf without any of my family noticing.

I had just parked my truck next to Stone's when the man himself walked out of the house and made a beeline toward me.

Fuck. There was no escape now.

"Good. You're just in time," Stone said.

"Just in time for what?"

"Meetin'."

Shit. It seemed like there was a meeting every frigging night of the week in this town. Planning board, zoning board, town, Grange, Rotary, Chamber—it was insane. And Morgan Farm was represented by at least one of us at them all.

I'd conveniently forgotten about this one.

Since I'd skipped last night's meeting because I'd been at Red's for dinner, I'd told Stone I'd go with him to tonight's.

"All right." I cursed my bad timing and sighed.

I needed to get out to the shed and feed that calf sometime soon but it wasn't going to happen now. I'd hoped to do it before dark, but it looked like I'd be sneaking out there with a flashlight later tonight, after the damn meeting. I just hoped no one saw me.

"Get in. I'll drive." Stone hooked a thumb at his truck, which meant I'd be at his mercy.

I wouldn't be able to slip out and escape big brother until we got home later. And cripes, I only hoped we were coming straight home and he wouldn't want to stop and toss a couple back at the bar first.

A brainstorm hit me. "My truck's already warm. Get in. I'll drive."

Stone nodded, seeing the value of a warm truck on a frigid winter evening.

We arrived just in time. The mayor banged the gavel for order just as Stone and I slipped in through the door. We stood along the back wall, our favorite place for these meetings. It would make for a quick escape the second this thing was over.

Settling in for an hour or so of small-town politics and griping by the old folk, I leaned against the wall and pulled out my cell. I figured this would be the perfect time to multitask. I could scroll through Facebook to see if there was anything new being said to Red while this bullshit meeting got underway.

"Cashel . . . I saw your truck parked there today. Did you see the calf?"

The sound of Mary Brimley saying my name had my head whipping up.

Absorbed in the black hole that was social media, I didn't know how long I'd been scrolling on my phone or what I'd missed.

Why was I suddenly part of this meeting? I was confused.

"Uh, what?" I asked.

I sounded like a dunce I'm sure but she'd not only taken me unaware, my mind was spinning wondering if it was obvious to everyone here that things had changed between Red and me.

Were my very vivid memories of what we'd just done written all over my face? Funny that I was most worried the town would find out about my fooling around with Red, when I should be more worried about the calf I'd taken and hid in the shed.

"I saw his truck at Red's too," Alice Mudd chimed in. "Did you see the calf while you were there?"

Stone turned toward me and waited for an answer along with the rest of the room.

I glanced at Stone, then addressed to two old biddies directly. "I stopped by the shop to see what was new on the mark down table. I didn't see the calf. It must not be on clearance yet." I lifted one shoulder and grinned.

Half the assembly chuckled at my attempt at a joke. The other half sent me dagger-filled glares. Yup, that seemed about right. Normal. Good. Nothing amiss here.

"Good excuse," Stone said low.

"Not a fucking excuse. It's true," I mumbled.

I had gone inside the shop. I had stood and pretended to look at the clearance table while that local piece of work laid into Red. No lie about all that.

"And how the fuck did they know it was my truck anyway and not yours or Boone's?" I continued, grumbling softly enough that only Stone could hear.

Dad had negotiated a deal with the local car lot and bought the three new farm trucks at the same time for a pretty nice savings. He'd cut a similar deal with the guy who lettered the Morgan Farm name and address on the doors. But that meant all three vehicles were nearly identical.

Stone cocked up a brow. "You're the one who put on that stupid bumper sticker."

Fuck. I'd forgotten about that. It said *Condoms prevent minivans.* I loved that sticker. It was both funny and true, but I might be willing to sacrifice it to get back my anonymity. I'd have to think about it.

Now that I was aware they were discussing Red and that calf, I pocketed my cell and paid some attention to the conversation.

"I have something to say." Old Buck raised his hand in the front row.

"Yes, Buck," Mayor Picket said, not even trying to hide his exasperation with the old man and his frequent interruptions and complaints at every meeting.

Being from the *older than dirt* generation, Buck always felt he needed to stand to officially address the assembly. The problem with that was it took him so long to get out of the chair we were all getting old just waiting on him.

"Burning daylight here," I mumbled under my breath as I waited what seemed like forever.

That earned me a wide-eyed censure from Stone as he hissed, "Shh."

I rolled my eyes at my shushing from big bro.

Finally, Buck was on his feet. "I don't agree with backyard livestock within the village proper. Never

157

have, never will."

We all knew what that was about. Buck fought tooth and nail to keep Agnes from being able to keep Petunia at her house.

Rumor had it Buck had been sweet on Agnes many, many years ago. Folks said she'd spurned his advances and that caused hard feelings between them that lived on to this day.

"Buck, we're not reversing the ruling on Petunia so don't even suggest it. But I do agree with you on this matter. Backyard chickens and even the pig were one thing, but a cow is a different story."

As I listened, I considered how ridiculous this conversation was. The calf in question was no longer at Red's place and no one in this room knew where it was so it was a moot point.

In the meantime, Boone slipped in the door and said, "Hey."

"Hey," I returned as Stone nodded to our tardy little brother.

"What'd I miss?" Boone hissed softly.

"Old man Buck is against keeping backyard livestock in the village," I filled in Boone as old lady Trout stood.

"I agree with Buck," Margaret Trout said. "If we let Red Meyer have a cow, what's next? Horses on Main Street?"

"Exactly. Or those alpacas that people are keeping nowadays," Alice Mudd agreed.

"Yes, I can see how it would be a slippery slope,"

Margaret commented. "Who knows what else people will want to keep in their yards next."

"Like llamas?" Boone suggested, loud enough for the old folks in the front to hear.

God, how I loved my little brother and his quietly rebellious streak. Following his lead, I said, "Or goats."

"Right." Boone nodded. "Or monkeys."

"Or emus," I added.

"What about ostrich?" he asked. "Wait. Are they the same as emus?"

"Not sure. I'll have to Google." Happy to be shining a light on the absurdity of this meeting, I whipped out my cell and made a show of googling the answer.

As I did Boone said, "You know, I read you can buy a zebra online."

"Really?" I exclaimed as I glanced up from my phone. "That'd be awesome."

The crack of the gavel ended our fun.

I glanced at Stone's face as he sighed, as if he were regretting our shared DNA.

Too bad. He'd get over the embarrassment. Besides, Stone should be on our side. On Red's side.

Sometimes the people in this town were ridiculous. Somebody needed to slap them, even if it was verbally. I was happy to be the man to do it.

Boone felt the same. Grinning, he bumped my fist with his, down low at my side where no one else would notice.

Let Stone be a fuddy duddy. The younger Morgan brothers were on the case.

The meeting continued. They talked ad nauseum about Red's calf. About how she'd illegally had it in her carriage house. The fact it was missing again and there was now a reward. And what would happen when it was found.

I didn't let it get me mad because they weren't going to find it. Not as long as I was around and I wasn't going anywhere.

The discussion moved to some other business, but it never got as interesting or amusing again as the backyard barn animal discussion had been earlier.

Next to me, Boone yawned, only covering his mouth after a glare from Stone.

Finally, the crack of the mayor's gavel shot Boone and I into motion. He made it through the back door first only because he was standing between me and it. But I was hot on his heels, skidding to a stop by the truck parked just down the block. He stopped too and we both glanced back to see Stone following behind at a little more leisurely pace but still striding away from the meeting fast enough to avoid getting caught in a conversation with one of the gabbers.

"Wanna hit up the bar?" Boone asked.

Shit. Exactly what I'd feared.

"I gotta head home. I've got some chores I didn't finish." I slipped in my lie before Stone reached us and might have questioned me.

Lucky for me Boone didn't question what chores or why I'd be doing them in the dark. Good boy.

"All right. Well come meet me later if you want," Boone offered.

"Sure. Maybe I will," I said.

Stone's arrival had me asking, "Ready? Don't wanna get stuck talking."

"True that." He glanced behind us at the oncoming hoard of shuffling seniors who would soon reach us on the sidewalk and want to talk. And talk. And talk some more.

Boone nodded and said, "See you later."

He took off at a trot to his truck parked a few spaced back from mine.

I skidded around the hood to the driver side as Stone climbed into the passenger seat and soon, we were on our way, veering into Main Street and hanging a tight U-turn to head for home.

"So Red have any idea where that calf got to?" Stone asked.

I glanced over to see if he was asking because he suspected, or simply because he was wondering. I didn't want to admit I'd just been at her place, any more than I wanted him to figure out I'd been the one to take the calf.

"Don't know. She say anything to Harper?" I asked.

Answer a question with a question—it was the best way to deflect Stone's trajectory. And mentioning his girl would only add to the smoke screen.

"All she said was the door was open so Carson thinks it got out."

Carson. Just the name had my grip tightening on the steering wheel.

Did he never have a day off? The damn deputy seemed to have taken Red on as his personal policing duty. It seemed any problem she had, he came running. I didn't like it. But I had to get over that and look at the bigger picture.

I glanced at Stone. "I guess if the sheriff's department thinks it escaped out the open door, then that must be what happened."

"But I mean, it escaped in the middle of the village. How long can it be before somebody sees it?" Stone asked.

"It could have worked its way down the side street and be hiding in the bushes along the river. I mean it needs water to drink. It might head that way." I was happy with my theory. It seemed conceivable even if it was complete bullshit.

But one thing was true. That calf was going to be hungry and thirsty by now and I needed to get rid of Stone, fill a bottle and feed her.

Luckily the fates were with me and Stone hopped into his own truck the moment we got home and headed out to see Harper. His being in love was making it a hell of a lot easier for me to get away with doing shit he wouldn't approve of. I liked it.

Yay, for love . . . for Stone, at least. Not for me.

In my observations, the L-word came with the R-word, as in relationship, which almost always led right into the P-word—pussy-whipped. Stone driving to Vestal so Harper could buy pajamas was proof of that.

I wasn't ready for any of those letters yet—

Was I?

No. Definitely not . . . Maybe.

Shit. I didn't know.

All I did know was that blowjob had been pretty incredible today. BJ. Now those were two letters I really liked.

My cunning wit had me chuckling to myself even if there was no one there to share it with as I proceeded with my stealth errand.

"Hey, girlie. How are you? I'm so sorry I'm so late. Your Uncle Stone was a pain in my ass and kidnapped me to a meeting."

I sat in the straw next to the calf. Cradling her head in my lap, I didn't have to do more than put the bottle near her mouth for her to latch on and start sucking down her dinner.

"Wow. You're hungry. Don't tell your mommy I let you go so long before feeding you."

My conversation with the calf had me thinking of Red, not that she'd been far from my mind before that.

She'd want to see her baby, I was sure. It might be too risky to have her visit in person right now. I wouldn't put it past the stock dealer to be keeping an eye on her. Suspicious fuck.

But I could definitely take a couple of pictures for

her.

Being the great multitasker that I was, I managed to keep feeding the calf while wrestling the cell out of my jeans pocket.

"Smile, pretty girl."

I snapped a couple of action shots, then admired my work on the display screen. I had to admit, she was a cutie.

"You're a real beauty, just like your beautiful momma Red," I said aloud and then realized something.

I wanted to see Red. Hell, I wanted to more than see her.

Yeah, it might ruin our friendship. But fuck the consequences. One taste of Red had only made me want more.

"Drink up, baby girl. I've got a lady I need to see tonight." And I had a bad feeling I wouldn't even try acting like a gentleman this time.

CHAPTER SIXTEEN

Red

I watched my cell phone's display light up. Once. Then again. And again.

The group text between Bethany, Harper and me was hopping.

I glanced at it quick to make sure nothing important was happening.

In this town, and with these women, you never knew. It could be anything. Intruder in the attic. Missing chickens. Bat in the kitchen. Harper had all three things happen to her over the period of a couple of weeks.

I never completely ignored the texts. But sometimes, like when I was busy with customers, I wouldn't reply. Or, like now, when I had no good reason but still had no intention of replying.

That decision was not because Harper and Bethany were comparing recipes and I, as a person who could cook but usually chose not to, had nothing to contribute.

I wasn't responding because I was afraid. Afraid one word from me, even by text, would tip off my two best friends that something life changing had just happened with Cash.

Yes, the world would keep turning. The Mudville gossip mill would keep churning. But my world as far as my relationship with Cash was forever altered and I wasn't sure that was a good thing.

No doubt the physical aspect had been good. Great. Amazing. But the rest? Him flying out of here. That sucked monkey butt.

But he'd also saved my calf from being returned to the meat pen at the stock auction—one more thing I had to hide from my friends—proving he was a good guy. A great guy.

For what he had done for me and that calf, in spite of it probably being larceny, or a felony, or something very bad that I wasn't really sure of, I would be forever grateful.

And so, I remained torn. About Cash. About changing my mind and participating in this discussion in my group chat that had now turned to something I actually had an opinion on—getting more followers on Instagram for each of our three respective businesses.

I was about to cave and suggest we do some sort of joint promotion involving my store, Harper's books and Bethany's baking, when there was a knock on my door.

My head whipped up. It could be the sheriff's department coming to question me about the calf.

And now that I actually knew where she was, they were the last people I wanted to speak to.

It could also be Cash.

"Red?" The sound of his voice had me untangling my legs from the throw on the sofa and running for the door.

Cell still in my hand since I'd forgotten to put it down in my excitement, I struggled to unlock the door. When I got it open, Cash was standing there, hands braced high on the doorframe, his head down until he lifted it to look at me.

He stared at me for a moment. Our gazes locked as his nostrils flared with his rapid breaths.

"This is bad. I shouldn't be here," he said.

I couldn't disagree more. "Why not?" I asked.

"I took some pictures for you of the calf eating."

"I'd love to see. But why is that bad?"

"Because I could have—I *should* have—texted them to you. But instead I came over because I wanted to see you."

I smiled. "I don't think that's bad at all."

He pressed his lips together, still hovering in the doorway.

His gaze dropped to the floor again as he said, "There's something else."

"Yeah?" I asked.

Cash brought his gaze back up to meet mine. He drew in a deep breath and said, "I've got a pocket full of condoms."

"A pocket full of condoms, huh?" I said, my lips twitching.

He wasn't exactly a Boy Scout, but at least he was prepared.

I had to bite my lip to keep from laughing. Partially from the miserable expression on his face at that admission. Partially from the fact he'd made the confession at all.

It was like the two sides of Cash—the good boy and the bad boy—were both equally strong. As if they coexisted side by side within him.

The bad side did what he wanted while the good side took care of the apologies and that made it all okay. And, I realized, I wanted both sides of him. I wanted him.

"Cash. Come inside."

He pushed off the doorframe, following me into the living room. I heard him close and lock the door but I didn't see it because I was walking toward my bedroom at the time.

In the doorway between the two rooms I paused and glanced back to where he stood, frozen in place, watching me.

"You coming?" I asked.

I saw his shocked expression at my invitation. Finally, he recovered. He smiled as he said, "Not yet, but I hope to be soon."

There was the bad boy I knew and loved. Just in time. Right when I needed him.

I put my cell on Do Not Disturb because, well, I

didn't want to be disturbed. Not during this.

Whatever was happening out in the real world could wait.

I was about to finally do what I'd dreamed about since my teen years. Have sex with Cashel Morgan. But instead of my teen imaginings, where we'd been everywhere from the back of his truck, to behind the bleachers on the ball field, this time we'd be in my bed. Like adults.

It was going to be great. I was considering exactly how great when two strong hands lifted me from behind and tossed me onto the mattress. He flipped me over onto my back before I could react and leaned low.

His fingers were already poised at the elastic waist of my pajama bottoms as he asked. "You ready?"

Ready for a near feral and aroused Cash? No, I suspected I was not. But I'd never admit that. Not to him. Not even to myself.

I nodded and that was all the prompting he needed.

My bottoms disappeared as he yanked them down my legs, off my feet, and tossed them onto the bedroom carpet. I was bare from the waist down, except for my fuzzy socks with the corny saying on the soles. *If you can read this, bring me a glass of wine.*

As Cash lowered his head between my legs and I had trouble breathing, I had to think I might need an oxygen mask instead of that wine.

He latched on to my core with a practiced expertise I tried not to think about too much.

No matter where he'd gotten his experience, I was the woman benefiting from it now. He was focused solely on me as he spread my thighs wide to accommodate his head.

He must have ditched his jacket sometime when I wasn't looking but he was still over dressed in a long-sleeved T-shirt, jeans and work boots.

I'd have to worry about getting him naked later. I was too busy trying not to sound like a bad porno now as Cash dragged out of me sounds I'd never made before. I wasn't ready for how hard and fast the orgasm would hit me.

Grasping his hair in my fists I rode his mouth like a bucking bull at the county fair.

When the spasms slowed and sanity returned, I finally released my hold on his hair.

Free of my tight grip, Cash glanced up, a crooked smile on his lips as he straightened. I watched as he kicked off his boots and pulled the T-shirt over his head.

The man should never wear a shirt ever. Not with muscles like that. Not bulky like gym rats and body builders. Leaner and oh so defined. *Farmer fit.* That was the perfect term, I decided as his hands moved to his belt and distracted me.

Before taking off his jeans, Cash proved he hadn't lied about the condoms when he reached into one pocket and tossed a handful on the bed. I stared at them until him pushing his jeans down his legs dragged my attention back to him.

His thighs were perfection, defined by long, hard

muscles that proved the man lifted with his legs while tossing all those bags of feed and bales of hay.

I was having a full out farmer fantasy for myself when Cash shoved his boxer briefs down his legs and that part I'd become intimately familiar with this afternoon sprang forward.

So smooth yet so hard, it held my attention completely. Rude maybe to be staring like this. I'd probably be angry if he stared at my boobs like I was at his cock, but I couldn't help myself. I was rapt as he reached for one condom, tore into the wrapper, and covered himself.

My heart pounded as he climbed over me to kneel between my legs on the bed, his eyes focused on mine.

His gaze dropped down as he dragged one fingertip down my slit and over highly sensitive nerves, shooting a tremor through me.

He looked up again and said, "This has been a long time coming."

"Yeah. It has," I agreed, though this seemed like an odd time to be starting a conversation.

Luckily, he was done with words as he lifted my knee with one hand and lined himself up with my entrance with the other.

The cutest crease formed between Cash's brows as he concentrated on his task.

When he pushed inside me, that thought and all others fled.

The one question that shot through my mind as

my body tingled in response to his was, why the heck had we waited so long?

CHAPTER SEVENTEEN

Cash

"I gotta get home."

Not that I really wanted to leave. Then again, I wasn't sure about staying either.

Having sex with a woman was one thing. Sleeping with her—as in actual slumber—was quite another.

Red and I were too new for that. Too good of friends and that part threw all sorts of complications into what we'd just done.

"Oh?" she said, struggling to sit up while still covering her tits with the sheet.

Why she was worried about exposing her nudity to me I had no clue.

I'd been the one to take off her shirt after round one. I'd had those nipples between my teeth as she came by my hand just before round two.

And if I didn't want to be hard as a rock again, I needed to stop thinking of all that. Swinging my legs over the side of the mattress, I stood.

I reached for my underwear and said, "Yeah. I don't want anybody to know where I am."

My hanging out with Red now, of all times, was a bad idea. Any number of people could make the connection. She had a calf go missing. My family owned a farm full of cows.

It was a risk I didn't want to take for all of our sakes, not in the least that little girlie hidden in the shed.

As I reached for my jeans I wondered exactly when it would be safe for me and the calf. Probably not until the damn thing was full sized and less recognizable since its picture had already been plastered on Facebook.

I reached for my shirt and turned to see Red, sitting up against the headboard with an odd expression on her face.

"You all right?" I asked.

"Just fine. Could you just maybe throw me my pants and top?"

Still with the modesty? I didn't question her but I did silently consider playing keep-a-way with her clothes just to see what she'd do.

The mature side of me won out and I said, "Sure."

I handed her the clothes and sat on the edge of the bed to put my boots back on, figuring turning my back to her would make her and her sudden bout of shyness feel more comfortable.

My cell vibrated in my pocket and I had to stand to pull it out. It was Boone, letting me know he was leaving the bar and heading home, just in case I'd been on the way to meet him.

Crap. If he beat me home, he'd see I was out, but not at the bar, and then the questions would follow. I had to get back fast.

Red was safely back in her PJs when I turned to her. "I, uh, gotta go."

"Okay." There was that tone again, putting an edge on a deceptively simple answer.

This was why I didn't date. Women should come with a handbook or a decoder ring. Then maybe I'd know what the hell they were thinking and feeling and what I was expected to do about it.

Was this because she wanted me to stay the night?

If that's what she really wanted then I'd have to figure something out for next time. Maybe sneak out of the house after everyone was asleep then sneak back in before anyone woke . . . and now I felt like I was back in high school again.

Maybe it was time I got my own place. Still, living with Mom and Dad had its benefits. Free rent. No commute to work. Laundry and meals provided.

I sighed. I'd figure it out, but not tonight.

"Walk me to the door?" I asked.

"Sure." Another one-word answer delivered in a tone that spoke volumes.

Yup. She was pissed.

We'd reached the door and the end of our time together.

With the clock ticking on Boone's arrival home, I didn't have long, so I put all my energy into grabbing her face between my hands and kissing her, hard and thorough. I took her mouth like a man who hadn't just taken her front ways and backwards just an hour ago.

When I finally let her go, she stumbled back a step. Her eyes looked a little unfocused and I knew my job was done here.

"See you tomorrow, beautiful." With a smile, I opened the door and ran down the stairs.

I'd purposely left the couple of extra condoms on her bed—for next time if all went well—so the only thing in my front pocket now was my truck key. I was about to pull it out when movement caught my eye.

Mother fucker. If I wasn't completely crazy it was the same size and shape as the shadowy figure I'd seen creeping around Red's yard last time. But this time, I'd seen him before he'd seen me.

As he reached into the big orange donated clothing bin set up at the end of the shop's driveway, I tackled him.

The guy didn't have a chance. It hadn't been that long since I'd played football and I was bigger and stronger now. Not to mention I was motivated. This was my girl he was fucking with and he wasn't going to get away with it again.

Not on my watch.

I had him pinned beneath me and was shouting questions at him beneath Red's motion light when I heard her voice, "Cash. Oh my God. What's going on?"

"Your thief is back. Call the sheriff."

Events moved quickly from there. It all felt like a big jumble of flashing lights and questions, both from the deputy—John Callahan this time instead of Carson—and from the neighbors.

The kid was put in cuffs and shoved in the back of the deputy vehicle. And he was indeed a kid.

The fact that it had turned out to be a boy— maybe thirteen or so—did much to deflate my superhero ego at having caught him. I probably outweighed him by about seventy pounds.

But young or not, he'd still been up to something tonight, and most likely the other night too. Proper procedure had to be followed.

"So how did you see him?" Callahan asked.

He'd graduated high school with Stone and had been such a fuck off back then, I was having trouble taking him seriously in his role of authority now.

Time for a lie.

"I was driving by on my way to meet Boone at the bar, when a text came through from him saying he was leaving and on his way home. So, I swung in the side street to turn around and head home again when movement caught my eye."

Damn, I was a good liar. Too bad a person couldn't make a living fibbing. Well, unless I wanted to be a politician.

I smothered a chuckle at that since this was serious business and continued, "Since Red has been having trouble with intruders, I parked down the block and snuck back just in time to see him messing with the donation box."

"You hear anything?" Callahan asked, looking past me.

I turned and saw Red was standing right behind me. Red shook her head in answer to Callahan's question.

She looked kind of shell shocked. I didn't blame her.

I'd have given anything to be able to pull her against me, wrap my arms around her and make her feel better, but that wasn't appropriate.

In the eyes of everyone here, we were just old friends from high school. Nothing else. I didn't want the town gossiping about us, so I could no more give her a hug than tell Callahan the truth—that I'd been leaving Red's apartment at almost eleven p.m. when I'd seen the guy.

"Anything of value taken?" he asked her.

"I don't know. I mean I haven't checked the shop. But if all he was doing was pawing through the bin, then no. There's nothing in there but clothing donations for charity. It's where I put the stuff I can't sell in the shop."

Callahan nodded then flipped his little book shut. "All right. Let me know if you discover anything missing." He turned to go and I stepped forward.

"Wait. What now? What are you going to do with him?"

Callahan glanced back. "Question him. See if I can find out who he belongs to. If I can't, lock him up and call social services in the morning."

I nodded and got a glimpse of the kid's face through the window of the vehicle. He looked scared shit.

As a kid who'd gotten into his share of trouble back in the day—and still could if my recent theft of the calf was any indication—I felt for the kid.

I'd have to stop by the department in the morning and see what had become of him.

Turning back after Callahan drove away, I was wishing the next-door neighbor who'd come out to see what was happening would go home so I could make sure Red was all right, just as Harper and Stone arrived. Apparently, Stone had been having a late night himself with Harper.

There'd be no alone time with Red again tonight. I'd have to check on her in the morning too after I got my chores done. But right now, I'd have to deal with Stone.

"What the fuck is going on?" he asked as he strode toward me.

I sighed. Yup. It was going to be a late night and an early morning.

CHAPTER EIGHTEEN

Red

Sleep did not come easy for me.

Not after I convinced Harper I would be fine alone and everyone finally left so I could get to my bed. Not as the sun began to rise and I started to lose hope I could get at least a few hours of sleep before having to get up and open the shop.

The night before kept playing through my mind. I remembered Cash's words verbatim. They still cut me to the core.

"Gotta get home. I don't want anybody to know where I am."

That gem came right before he lied on an official sheriff's report by saying he'd been driving by rather than say he'd been at my place.

I could have forgiven the second transgression if not for the first. I could have explained his lie to Callahan by his not wanting to feed town gossip. His attempt to not embarrass me for having a man in my apartment at close to midnight. But that first comment delivered to me in private as he ran out of my bed rather than stay the night . . .

Yeah, that hurt.

I'd thought I could be happy with what we were. Friends with benefits. But the more I thought about it, the angrier I got. I didn't want to be any man's dirty little secret.

I suppose I should be happy to be friends with benefits with Cash.

Some would say it was the best of both worlds. I could keep the old friendship and enjoy the new benefits. And considering how much I'd enjoyed those benefits, more than once, I really should be satisfied.

So how come I wasn't?

Then there was that kid Callahan had cuffed and driven away last night. He seemed so young. Too young to be a habitual criminal.

I wasn't naïve. I knew he could be hooked on drugs or involved in some bad shit, even at that young age. But he could also just be a kid down on his luck. What had he really taken from me? A cape and a sleeping bag. Some old clothes out of the donation bin.

There'd been a year during my childhood when times had been tough. The adults tried to hide the full extent of it from me and my older sister, but I had no doubt we were never too far from being homeless before things finally turned around for us.

All I knew was I needed to find out either way. And if I was going to do that and still get the store opened on time, I had to get to the sheriff's department early.

Since I wasn't getting any sleep anyway, I changed out of my PJs. Not that I needed to have bothered. The whole neighborhood had seen my pajamas in the driveway last night anyway. But I put on clothes good enough to go to work in later and fired up the truck.

John Callahan had the night shift, so I figured Carson should be on this morning. That was good. Carson would be more likely to share the information I wanted than his slightly older, and so much crankier co-worker.

"Hey. Good morning," I said when I saw him at his desk.

He cocked a brow and stood. "Good morning. You're up early considering the night you had."

For a split second I thought he was talking about what happened with me and Cash, before common sense took over and I realized he was talking about the kid.

"You heard?" I asked.

"John gave me a quick rundown during shift change and then I read the rest in the report." Carson's lips quirked up in a crooked smile. "So, lucky for you that Cashel was *just driving by* your place at eleven p.m., huh?"

Crud. He *had* been talking about me and Cash. At least partially. I opened my mouth to deny it but didn't get a chance.

Carson held up one hand. "Look, you don't have to admit anything to me. Just, I mean if you two are dating, you know, come out with it already. What are you hiding it for? You're single. He's single."

The problem wasn't me. It was most definitely him. Though, maybe partially me too, but only because of him.

It was my fear that he wasn't in this for anything more than a little sex that made me not want anyone to know. Otherwise, I might have been convinced to give having a serious relationship with Cashel Morgan a try.

Just thinking those words—a serious relationship with Cash—sounded ridiculous in my head.

What was I thinking? He was the class clown in high school. And the town flirt after graduation. The guy who didn't have a girlfriend, but no doubt had plenty of girls.

I sighed. Nope. It was a fling. A one-night stand and now it was over.

Nothing I could do about that, but maybe there was something I could do about the kid from last night.

"Cash and I are never going to be more than what we are now," I said. "And since we already have the old biddies for town gossip and they don't need any help from the sheriff's department, can we get to what I came here for?"

Carson's brows shot up and I realized that all had come out sounding a lot nastier than I'd intended. With half the town hating me over that calf, I really shouldn't alienate the few friends I had left.

I shook my head. "I'm sorry. I didn't sleep. I'm

exhausted and cranky and not a very nice person right now. I shouldn't have taken it out on you."

He shook his head. "No. I should apologize to you. You're right. I need to mind my own business. And stop mixing work and personal."

I drew in a breath. "So, I wanted to ask about the kid from last night."

"Yeah." Carson blew out a loud sigh. "That's a tough one."

"In what way? I know nothing about him. Were you able to find his parents?"

"We found nothing. He had no ID on him and he's refusing to give us a name or address. That means we're stuck pawing through the system looking for a match among reports of missing children."

"Wow."

"Yeah. The way it stands now we're waiting for child services to arrive and hoping to find him a spot somewhere. Juvenile facilities are over-crowded. And even temporary placements with a foster family are hard to come by. Not that I'm convinced we should be sending him to live with a family given the fact that if he is your thief, he's been making a habit of break-ins all over this town. Your shop. The old Van de Berg house. Your place last night."

I nodded, wishing I could help and knowing I couldn't.

"You want a cup of coffee? It's actually pretty decent from the new maker the sheriff sprung for. You look like you could use it."

Two things prompted me to say no to that. One, I needed to get back and open the store. And more importantly, a big pick-up truck that I would bet money had the words *Morgan Farm* painted on the door had just pulled into the lot. And I had no doubt it would be Cash behind the wheel.

Since he couldn't wait to get away from me last night so no one would know he'd been at my place, I figured I'd do him a favor and get out of here now. Wouldn't want to compromise his big secret. Make that his dirty little secret—me.

"No. Thank you though. I gotta get to the shop."

Wishing there was a back door I could slip out without looking like a lunatic in front of Carson, the next best thing I could do was get out of there and into my truck as quickly as possible.

"All right. I'll keep you informed with what's going on."

"Thanks. I appreciate that, Carson."

I really did. Carson was a really good guy. And once again, I wished I felt for the deputy even half the attraction I felt for Cash.

Chalk that up to my bad taste in men, I guess. I didn't have time to come up with any other reason for it right now.

I headed for the door faster than a normal person would but that couldn't be helped. As it was, Cash was already out of his truck and walking toward the building when I skipped down the stairs.

"Red—" Cash began.

"Hey. Running late. Gotta go." I waved without making eye contact and climbed into the truck.

Holding my breath, I turned the key in the ignition and prayed my old girl would start. The dead last thing I needed right now was Cash feeling like he had to help me fix my truck, or Carson seeing him doing it.

She started up just fine and I counted that as a good sign. Maybe my luck was changing.

It certainly couldn't get any worse.

CHAPTER NINETEEN

Cash

Having watched Red drive away—after barely saying *hello* to me—I walked into the sheriff's department and faced the man who had become my nemesis.

Carson Bekker.

I shouldn't be surprised to see him. The man worked here. And there was no doubt in my mind Red was here about the kid they'd arrested last night. But still, Carson kept turning up with Red, like a bad penny.

I had to remind myself it had been me in Red's bed last night. Not Carson.

The way Red was acting so weird, that was little consolation. I was having a hard time feeling like the winner.

"Well, look at this. The second party has arrived," Carson said.

"Second party—what?" I asked, confused and already annoyed with Carson's cocky smile.

"The two parties named in the report from last night. Red was just here."

"I know. I saw her." That came out more defensively than I'd meant.

Carson's brow rose but he continued as if I hadn't spoken, "And now, you're here. I'm going to assume also to inquire about the kid and if we found out anything about him."

"Yeah. Actually."

He lifted his shoulders. "I'm gonna tell you the same thing I told her. We've got nothing. No identification. Nothing when we run his prints. And he's not talking back there." Carson hooked a thumb toward the back.

I couldn't see the cells but knew they were there. I might have spent a night in one once. Boys will be boys.

But his comment told me a lot. The boy hadn't already been sent off with child services. "He's still here?"

"Yup."

"Could I possibly talk to him?" I hated asking for a favor, especially since I'd been nothing but a dick toward Carson for days. He'd have every right to say no and I guess I couldn't blame him.

He stared at me for a second before he said, "Sure. Come on back."

"Really? Thanks."

Carson grabbed a set of keys from the drawer and I followed him back.

Hopefully he wouldn't lock me in with the kid and conveniently forget about me for a few hours as retaliation. That might be something I would do—as a joke, of course.

Not Carson. As much as it pained me to say it, Carson was a good guy.

"Sit down in there. I'll bring him to you." He tipped his chin toward an interrogation room.

I went in and sat, looking around. I hadn't been in this room that night so it was new to me.

The sound of the door opening had me turning as Carson perp walked the kid into the room and pushed him by the shoulder down into the chair opposite me.

That seemed a little rough considering, even though the kid did have a *fuck you* expression firmly etched on his young face.

He reminded me a little bit of myself back then. I liked to joke around, but I really didn't like getting in trouble for it. I hated authority.

Carson stood by the door with his arms folded. Apparently, he'd be chaperoning. That was fine. All I wanted was a few answers.

A phone ringing out in the office area had Carson mouthing a curse. "I'm the only one here at the moment. I gotta get that."

"That's fine. We're good," I said, eyeing the kid.

I'd taken him down once. I had no doubt I could do it again if need be.

Looking hesitant, Carson nodded and said, "Knock when you're done."

"Will do."

I folded my arms as the door clicked shut. The kid remained stone-faced and silent.

"What's up?" I asked, playing it cool.

"Not much. What's up with you, grandpa?"

Grandpa? I choked out a short laugh. So that's how this was going to go.

After a life of rebellion against the older folks in town, I had somehow become one of them. At least in the eyes of this kid.

Although I couldn't argue that now that I saw the boy in daylight, he was young enough I could have been his father.

"Wanna tell me what you were doing at Red's last night?"

"Wanna tell me what you were doing sneaking out of her place in the middle of the night? Oh, wait, you don't have to tell me. I heard what was going on."

"Bull shit." And now I was arguing with a kid. But still, he had me concerned.

"*Oh, yes. Yes, yes. Right there. Right there.*" He did a high-pitched imitation of Red and fuck me if I didn't remember her saying something just like that. "*Oh, fuck. Yeah. Red. Yeah, fuck. You're so tight.*" He'd moved on to an unflattering and inaccurate—I hoped— imitation of what I guessed was supposed to be me.

Christ. Was that what I sounded like? And did I really say all that to Red in the heat of the moment? No. He had to be lying.

I narrowed my eyes at him. "You didn't hear shit."

He lifted his shoulders and looked unconcerned.

"I came here to help you, you know," I told the little brat.

"You should have left me alone then if you really wanted to help me."

"Last night? So you could continue to squat in vacant houses and steal clothes?"

He shrugged again. "We were doing fine on our own until you."

We.

The word caught my attention. "We who? Who were you with? Is there somebody else still out there?" I asked.

He paled when he realized his mistake but tried to cover it with a scowl. "No. Just shut up, grandpa."

"Look. Joke all you want but I know you. I was the kid who got in all the trouble at your age. I was in one of those jail cells back there once."

"Oh, so this is where we're supposed to bond and I tell you my life story? Fuck that."

I drew in a breath and stood. Time for some scared straight, tough love. I was out of options. "Fine. Stay here. I don't care. As long as you're locked up, I know you won't be bothering Red. That's all I really care about anyway."

"Yeah. It sounded like you really cared last night."

I shook my head and let out a snort. "Whatever."

I moved toward the door, hoping that would spur the kid to talk. If it didn't, then this kid was a harder nut to crack than I'd thought and I was going to have to actually knock to get Carson's attention and leave.

"You really want to help?" he asked at my back.

I was almost afraid to turn around. I might look too eager and scare him off, so I didn't. I stayed facing the door, my hands at my side. "Depends what you're asking me to do, I suppose."

"Judging by your truck and your shit-kicking boots, I figure you're some sort of farmer. With animals maybe."

The kid sure knew how to lob an insult. I couldn't help the glance down at my barn boots.

"Yeah," I said, daring now to pivot half a turn to glance at him.

"There's an old yellow warehouse along the train tracks."

"I know the place." I nodded.

"There's a puppy tied up inside. He had food and water yesterday, but it's been a long time. And it's cold in there."

I swallowed, more affected than I'd planned on.

The kid might be a cocky bastard but he was an animal lover. Willing to put our little feud aside to ask for help for that dog. A kid like that couldn't be all bad.

"I'll go get him."

"You're not gonna bring him to the pound, are you? They'll put him down if he's there too long."

Fuck, now I was starting to like this little

troublemaker. "No, I won't bring him to the pound. I'll bring him home with me."

"To the farm?"

"Yeah, to the farm."

He nodded, then focused on the table.

I tried one more time to get something out of him. "You sure you don't want Carson to call your parents so you can get out of here?"

"Oh, yeah. Good idea. Why didn't I think of that?" The kid rolled his eyes at me.

"Do you not have parents?" I asked.

He turned his head and didn't answer, but I thought I saw tears in his eyes.

The conversation was over, but this kid's problems were just beginning. I wasn't sure what I could do about that, except go save his dog. So that was what I was going to do.

CHAPTER TWENTY

Red

When it rains, it pours.

I never really thought much about that saying. Mostly because I hate rain. But also, because I'm too damn busy treading water with my business to ponder old clichés.

But as I sat idling in the truck where I'd pulled over along the side of the road to take a call, I had to think I was currently under a deluge.

My life had gone on pretty much unchanged for months. Years really. No excitement. No dates. And now, something happened pretty much daily. Things lost and then found. Break-ins. Carson. Cows. Cashel. Dates. Dinners. Sex.

And now, this.

"Frank. This is crazy." Crazy I hadn't talked to this man in close to a year. Not since the last resellers conference I'd attended. Even more crazy that I was actually considering his offer.

"It is. Which is why I thought of you." I heard the

smile in his voice. "Do you have a valid passport or not?"

"I do." Only because I'd gotten it for my sister's thirtieth birthday trip to Cancun two years ago.

"So . . ." he prompted.

I repeated what he'd told me again, still not believing it. "Paris. Seriously?"

"Seriously," he said.

"How can I justify going to Paris for Haute Couture Week? I run a resale shop in Mudville, New York."

"I do believe I remember you bragging about your stock of Chanel shoes last I saw you. And wasn't there a Louis Vuitton purse or two on your shop's Instagram just last week?"

"Yes," I admitted. "But the flight leaves tomorrow?" I'd been known to do things spur of the moment, but even I thought that was insanely close.

"Tomorrow night, which gives you all day today and tomorrow to get ready."

"But how can you change the airline reservation?" I was pretty sure the airlines were not keen on swapping names on tickets for security reasons since what had happened on September eleventh.

"Didn't I tell you? We ended up getting a private jet for the group."

"No!" I exclaimed.

I was beginning to remember why I'd deleted the email about this trip a year ago when they'd been in the planning stages. The group was going all out and I knew it was going to be expensive.

"Yes!" he repeated with the same amount of enthusiasm I'd used. "Split thirty ways it wasn't all that much more than all of us booking flights individually. All you have to do, Miss Red, is get your pretty little self down to Kennedy Airport by tomorrow night at seven. Can you do that?"

I could. JFK wasn't close, but it was definitely drivable from upstate.

"But I have to pay you—"

"I told you. The trip is all paid for. Claudine dropped out, knowing it was non-refundable. Her share of the plane. Her hotel room. Her tickets to the fashion shows. The dinner under the Eiffel Tower. Even her shopping bus excursion and the tour and tasting at Veuve Clicquot—all paid for."

Claudine ran a very fancy resale shop in New Orleans. All high-end name brands. I might get in the occasional Chanel or Louis, but I could pretty much guarantee she never had chain saws or camo hunting gear come into her place the way I did.

Still, she'd paid a lot for a trip she wasn't even going on.

"Then I should pay her . . ."

"Stop! I'm sure she's already written the cost off on last year's taxes. All you'll have to come up with for the week is the money for incidentals. A few meals here and there. Drinks. Souvenirs."

That wasn't all I'd have to come up with. I'd have to come up with staff for my shop to cover my shifts while I was gone too. Otherwise I'd have to close.

That would lose me money and incur the wrath of shoppers who seemed to take it as a personal affront when I closed the shop for bad weather or a holiday.

But wait. I think the high school went on mid-winter recess this week. Gretchen would be off from school, though whether she'd want to spend her vacation working for me was another story.

Still, she was saving money to buy a car. She might want the extra hours. This trip might actually be possible.

"Does this silence mean you're thinking about it?" Frank asked.

"Yes, darn you."

He laughed. "Good to hear I can still persuade a pretty lady."

I sighed. Frank and I flirted, but that was all it was. All it had ever been for the five years I'd known him. Frank was a friend. A friend I did not have benefits with—unlike the situation with Cash.

Given how badly that whole thing with Cash made me feel, I don't think I'd be keen to try the friends with benefits thing again with anyone else real soon. If ever. But Paris with Frank and a group of twenty-eight other resale professionals? That I could do.

My heart raced with the thought of it, even as my mind spun with all the details I'd have to manage if I made this decision.

"What would I even pack to wear for a fashion show in Paris?" I asked.

"First of all, you do own a store full of outfits. But

besides that, you be you. Everyone loves your quirky self. You know that."

Quirky. I couldn't deny that. And I had been called worse—very recently in fact.

I drew in a loud breath and let it out. "How long can I take to decide and let you know?"

"I guess if you let me know by lunchtime today that'd be good. If you say no, I'll invite Angelica. I really would rather not, though, so please, just say yes."

It was after nine now.

I had to call Gretchen and find out if she could cover the shop or not. And of course, I had to open today for customers at ten, while trying to choose outfits and pack a suitcase and find my passport.

It was a lot. Even so, a part of me really wanted to do it.

"Okay. I'll call you back."

"All right. I have faith in you, Red. You'll make this work. And we're gonna have a great time. Talk to you soon."

"All right. Bye." I disconnected and sat for a second with the cell in my hand. Still shocked.

I wanted to believe him that I could make this work, even as my head spun with To-Do lists, the thought of which spurred me into action.

Was I crazy? I needed to run this by an impartial judge or two. I hit Harper's number in my contacts list.

When she answered ,I asked, "Any way you can

meet me at Bethany's right now? I have sort of an emergency and I need both of your help."

"Of course. Give me two minutes to throw on clothes and I'll see you there."

That's what I loved about Harper. No questions. Just action.

I slammed my foot down on the clutch, threw the truck in gear and hit the gas. Five minutes later, maybe six, I was armed with an extra tall cup of coffee, a sticky bun that I probably shouldn't be eating, and my two friends.

"So what do I do?" I asked.

"Why are you even questioning it? If a guy invited me to Paris, I'd go," Bethany said, coming around from behind the glass display case where she'd just finished waiting on a customer.

Now that the older woman had left, it was just us in the shop. And I was glad of that after Bethany's baseless insinuation about Frank.

I rolled my eyes. "It's not a guy inviting me to go. It's the event coordinator of the organization—who happens to be a man—inviting me, a member, to go. And if I don't go, he'll just invite someone else."

"Mmm, hmm. Sure." Bethany nodded, sounding sarcastic. "Except that he's hot."

"Is he?" Harper's eyes lit up.

I leveled a glare on Bethany. "How in the world do you know what he looks like?"

"I saw pictures of you two looking cozy together at that convention last year."

"Oh, really?" Harper's brows rose and she focused on me.

I remembered the picture she was talking about.

We'd all gotten a little drunk at a bar in Texas that last convention. The selfies were snapping that night, but nothing else happened.

I had no intention of starting something—emotional or physical—with a man who lived on the other coast. Especially one I had a professional relationship with.

I sighed. I didn't have time for this. And I really didn't have the energy for it. I was running on no sleep and the forecast for getting any in the near future looked slim to none.

"Frank and I are just friends," I said, for not the first time and I was sure not for the last. "But that's not the point. It feels so . . . extravagant. I can't actually go, can I?"

"Yes, you can." Harper's tone left no doubt of her stance on the matter. Bethany's enthusiastic nodding only reinforced Harper's opinion.

"It's too short notice," I said.

"It's all expenses paid," Bethany countered.

"The store—"

"Will be covered," Harper said, cutting off my next protest. "Whatever hours Gretchen can't take, I will."

"You?" My eyes widened.

I loved Harper but she was a bit of a hermit, going a full week without leaving the house sometimes. I

203

couldn't picture her up and out, dealing with customers. Especially some of *my* customers.

"Hey. I wasn't always an author. I worked retail for years. Food service too, in case you ever need me to cater a party or mix up some drinks."

"You are a jack of all trades, aren't you?" Bethany laughed.

"Ask her about her snobby museum job, one day," I said.

Harper leveled a glare on me. "You're changing the subject. Go, Red. It's once in a lifetime. When will you ever get the opportunity to do something this amazing again?"

"I agree." Bethany nodded. "Just do it. You'll regret it forever if you don't."

The worst part was I knew they were right. Not just about this amazing once in a lifetime trip. The timing really couldn't be better for me to get away from Mudville, even for just a week.

While I was gone, I'd escape the worst of the calf fall-out, not to mention the awkward post-sex period with Cash.

"Okay. I will. I'm gonna go."

Bethany jumped up to hug me while Harper clapped her hands.

"But this means I have to get moving. Like now. There are a hundred things to do."

"Text if you need anything. To borrow a suitcase. Me to watch the shop while you pack. Whatever," Harper offered.

"Okay, thank you." But there was something else I had to do before I left, and no one could do it except for me.

With my coffee cup shoved between my seat and the door, because vintage trucks don't have cup holders, I took out my cell phone and hit to dial the sheriff's department.

"Mudville Sheriff's Department, Deputy Bekker speaking."

"Carson, it's Red."

"Red, well, lucky me gets to talk to you twice in one day. Actually, it's good you called. We've got a court date for the kid. It's Monday morning at nine. I figured you'd want to be there."

Wow. Things moved fast in our county's legal system.

"Actually, that's why I'm calling. I'm uh going out of town unexpectedly for a week so I won't be around for the court date. But is there any way I can leave a statement with you, or officially drop any charges against him?"

"What? You sure you want to do that, Red? All evidence points to him being the one who broke in your store."

"I know. But, Carson, he's just a kid. I've made up my mind. I don't want to press charges and if it will help, I'll email over a letter asking the judge for leniency."

Carson sighed. "Okay. If that's what you want to do."

205

"It is."

"All right. I'll text you the email address."

"Thanks."

"And Red. Be careful in Paris."

"What the—How do you know?" I'd only made the decision a minute ago. Even the Mudville gossip network couldn't work that fast.

"Mary Brimley." He laughed.

"No. Come on. Seriously? How did she find out?"

"Well, near as I can tell, her friend was in the bakeshop while you were in there talking about your trip. She was on her way to pick up Mary to come here to drop off the donations for the coat drive."

"I'm surprised you managed to get rid of them so fast."

"Oh, I didn't. They're still here, bending the sheriff's ear about anything and everything. In fact, thanks for calling. Answering the phone was a good excuse for me to bow out of that never-ending conversation."

I laughed. "I bet. But I'm sorry to tell you I have to get off the phone and take care of business."

"That's okay. I'll just pretend we're still talking." He chuckled. "But I'm serious. Take care while you're abroad. I'll be sure to keep an eye on your place while you're gone. And I'll make sure Callahan knows to do some extra drive-bys."

"Thanks, but I think Mary and her network of spies has keeping an eye on things covered."

Carson laughed. "No kidding."

Still amazed by the twisted workings of Mudville society, I said goodbye to Carson, disconnected the call and let out a deep breath. I was already exhausted and now it was time to get to the shop and open the doors.

Meanwhile, since I was really doing this—really going on this whirlwind trip to Paris, I had one task completed, but about ninety-nine more to go.

CHAPTER TWENTY-ONE

Cash

I drove to the warehouse not knowing what to expect. I was prepared for the possibility that the kid had sent me on a wild goose chase but it was a chance I was willing to take. No dog deserved to be tied up alone for days.

What I found inside would tell me a lot about the still nameless kid. I'd soon know if he was a lying smart ass or really an animal lover. I braced myself for any of the possibilities as I slowed to a stop in front of the warehouse.

I evaluated how best to enter the abandoned building. The kid had been getting in and out, so I should be able to find a way in too.

Pocketing my keys, I began my walk around the perimeter. I tried the door and found it locked. But around back, a ground floor window looked part-way open.

I planted two hands on the sash and pushed. It wasn't easy but it finally gave way and moved.

Great. Now I'd get the pleasure of doing something I hadn't done since I was a teenager—crawling through a window.

I wasn't as slim or as light as I used to be. Good thing there was no one around to hear my grunting and groaning at the effort it took to get myself through.

Inside, I realized how dark a building with mostly boarded up windows could be, even in daytime.

There was no way I was going back out through the window to the truck to grab a flashlight. My cell phone was all I had with me so the flashlight feature was going to have to do.

I moved farther inside, looking for something, anything, to prove I hadn't been sent on a fool's errand.

Then I heard the soft whine. Then a bark.

Throat tight, I strode toward the noise, hoping I didn't find the pup in a bad way.

"Where are you, good boy?" I spoke as I walked, still not seeing the dog.

I found him easily enough once he heard my voice and started to really bark. I got my first look at the puppy, bouncing up and down while tethered by a rope. He was in a corner, tied to a radiator.

"Shh. Okay. Now you'd better be quiet before someone hears you and calls that mean Mudville Animal Control officer."

I moved closer and squatted down, right next to him so he would stop choking himself trying to get to me.

"Are you all right?" I asked, running my hands over his tiny body.

He felt cold but that was no surprise. It looked like the kid had set up a bed for them out of tarps, a blanket and some old clothes. The pup, tied and without any other choice, had peed on the pile. I could smell it and feel it soaking into the knee of my jeans where I kneeled.

Shining the light around I saw a bowl of water that had frozen over and a couple of open cans of food that had been licked clean.

I could see the kid had tried to care for the dog, but with him gone overnight, the pup was lucky I was here now.

Moving the beam of the flashlight to the radiator, I saw how the knot was tied and decided to not waste time trying to undo it. Instead I took out my pocketknife and cut the rope, but kept the end in my hand so the puppy didn't take off. I didn't feel like a chase.

I needn't have worried. It seemed the dog had taken a liking to me. The way he was bouncing around my legs, it was impossible to even stand up without tripping on him. Never mind walk.

Scooping him up, I cuddled him close to my chest. The mutt was maybe three months old. Small but with potential to be a big dog once he was an adult. Maybe a Labrador mix. Maybe a little Shepard in there.

It didn't matter what kind he was or how big he'd

grow to be, it looked like he was mine now. Just like the calf.

I seem to have acquired possession of two strays in two days. At this rate maybe I should open a sanctuary. Maybe try and get some tax breaks for all this animal rescuing I was doing.

Meanwhile by the time I was halfway home the puppy had already stolen my heart by insisting on sitting in my lap while I tried to drive.

No matter how many times I put him back in the passenger seat he crawled back over to me. I finally gave up and drove one handed. Good thing the truck was an automatic and the farm was close by.

What I was going to do with him when I got home was another story.

Unlike the calf, the puppy wasn't on the lam from the stock auction. At least, not that I knew of. I didn't have to hide him. But that also meant I'd have to tell my parents we now had a new dog.

We'd had to say goodbye to our old herding dog last year after fourteen years of having him. I figured it was about time the Morgans let a new dog into our lives anyway.

"What are we going to call you?" I asked the puppy as I slowed to pull into the drive. "Should we take a family vote? Or do I get naming privileges since I'm the one who had to carry you out the window? Huh?"

He didn't have any answers, but that was okay because he had plenty of tail wags and face licks for me instead.

Inside, I was surprised to find I had the kitchen to myself. That was better, actually. At least I'd have time to tend to the pup before I had to deal with explaining him to the family.

The first order of business was a bowl of water, which the puppy lapped up for a solid five minutes, in between glancing up to make sure I hadn't left him alone. Abandonment issues for sure.

"You gonna need some doggy therapy?" I asked him as I slid a plate of leftovers from last night's dinner onto the floor. "I'll get you some proper dog food at the store later. Until then, it's Morgan steak for you. Eat up. And don't tell Dad."

The dog seemed to appreciate the steak, but then again, he was likely starving.

"Don't tell Dad what?"

I glanced up and saw Boone. I tipped my head toward the pup. "We have a new family member. And he's fond of steak."

"Oh my God. Who is this little guy?"

"He's a stray. Found him tied up at the old factory along the tracks. What kind of reception you think he's going to get from Mom and Dad?" I asked, after skirting around the full truth about the origin of the pup.

"Oh, they're gonna love him because I already do." Boone was already on the floor, rubbing the pup's ears.

One family member won over. Three more to go.

"Um, what is that?" Stone asked from the

doorway.

I turned around from the junk drawer where I'd been searching for our old dog's choke collar to see Stone's frown.

Boone glared up at him from the floor. "It's a puppy and I love him and we're keeping him."

Had I traveled backward in time? I swear, judging by the conversation, if I saw a seven-year old Boone on the floor and a broody teenaged Stone in the doorway I wouldn't have been surprised at all.

"He needs a home. We've got a home." I shrugged.

"And what's a farm with no dog?" Boone asked.

"He doesn't look like a farm dog to me." Stone cocked up a brow.

"Any dog can be a farm dog," Boone shot back, the puppy in his lap now that he'd finished his meal.

"If he bothers the herd—"

"He won't. We'll train him," Boone promised Stone.

Stone still looked skeptical so I decided to bring out the big guns. "You keep picking on this poor pup and I swear, I'll tell your girlfriend. We'll see what she has to say about your anti-puppy attitude."

I knew exactly what would happen. Harper the animal lover would lay into Stone and then probably cut him off.

In fact, I might tell her just for fun, whether Stone straightened up or not. He'd been getting more sex than any man deserved lately anyway.

He rolled his eyes. "We'll see what Mom and Dad have to say."

I shook my head, the decision already made.

"Fine. But I'll move out and take him with me if I have to. Maybe it's about time I get my own place anyway. I'm turning thirty soon enough. That's a little old to be still living under my parents' roof. Don't you think?" I made sure to shoot Stone, who was about to turn thirty-two, a meaningful glance.

"Stop. Both of you. Ain't nobody moving out and leaving me here alone with Mom and Dad." Boone shot a glance at both of us. "Besides, they're gonna love this little guy. How can they not?"

"What's his name?" Stone asked.

I lifted a shoulder. "Doesn't have one that I know of."

"Well, better give him one. It's harder to get rid of an animal once it's got a name."

I smiled at Stone. The man did have a soft spot in his heart. He just hid it behind being an ass most times.

"Okay. So, any ideas?" I asked.

Boone was trying to answer but kept getting a mouth full of puppy tongue as he did and I was laughing too hard to think of something.

Even Stone let out a chuckle. "How about Romeo, since he's such a big kisser?"

"I like it." I grinned. "Boone?"

He nodded and finally gave me a thumb's up as he fought against the puppy and tried to wipe the saliva off his face with his shirt.

"Romeo it is." I'd found the collar and carried it over to the puppy, slipping it over his wiggly head. "I dub thee Romeo."

"You better get him his shots and a license or the animal warden will be knocking on the door with a fine for you for having an unlicensed dog," Stone warned.

I groaned as Boone nodded. "It's true. They're nuts with the rules in this town."

"I know, it's true." I'd paid the last fine we got because Duke's license had expired and the damn warden came knocking.

"We gotta get him fixed too," Boone added, still playing defense against the puppy attack.

Drawing in a breath, I began realizing exactly how much responsibility I'd just taken on. "I'll call and get an appointment for him."

I watched as the pup decided now was the time to gnaw on Boone's finger. The little guy looked up and saw me staring at him. And damned if the little thing didn't scurry over to me and try to climb up my leg.

"You want to get picked up, little guy?"

He wiggled in my arms, so happy I had to laugh. Yeah, he'd be a lot of work, but he was well worth it.

He was part of the family now. It didn't seem to matter what Mom and Dad said when they finally got in from wherever they were.

I only wished I could get the kid situated this easily. A dog was one thing. Even a cow was within my abilities. But a kid? That was bigger job than I was equipped to handle.

Or was it?

"Hey, you two know anyone who takes in foster kids around here?" I asked.

Stone frowned. "No. I don't think so."

"Me either." Boone shook his head, finally able to get off the floor since the puppy was now snoring in my arms. "But you know Bethany was a foster kid, right?" he said as he stood.

My eyes widened. "No, I did not know that."

"Why are you asking about foster kids?" Stone asked.

"I'll tell you later." I glanced at the sleeping pup and then up at Boone. "You okay taking care of him for a bit? I got an errand to run."

"Sure." He nodded and moved closer to take the puppy from me. "And I stashed all of Duke's old stuff in the attic. His bed. His bowls. I can bring it downstairs and set up Romeo in the pantry for now, with some newspapers in case he has an accident."

Preparing for an accident was probably wise. "Perfect. I'll pick up dog food while I'm out."

"And toys," Boone added. "He's gonna need something to play with and chew on. He's probably teething."

Stone nodded. "Yeah, something to chew on that's not the furniture if you have any hope of keeping him indoors."

"Gotcha. I'll get food and toys." And hopefully I'd

get some answers from Bethany so I could do something to help this kid.

He certainly seemed to need a little help for himself because if nothing changed, it looked as if social services was sending him off to some sort of facility.

Call me stupid, but I wasn't giving up on him yet. I had a gut feeling about this kid.

He might be in trouble and having problems at the moment, but I honestly didn't think he was a bad kid.

Anybody who loved animals couldn't be all bad. I only hoped he proved my instincts correct.

CHAPTER TWENTY-TWO

Red

"Just the carry-on bag? You sure you don't want to borrow one of my big suitcases?" Harper asked.

"No. I'm just bringing the one small bag."

"What if you buy stuff?"

"Like what? A few pair of Louboutin pumps? Maybe a Chanel dress or two? A Hermes bag?" I laughed. First that she thought I had that kind of money to spend on myself. Second, that anything so frivolous would be useful to me.

I lived in Mudville, for goodness sake. No formal wear required. The couple of times a year I traveled for business I could get anything I needed from my store.

Harper sighed. "I wish I was going with you."

I tipped my head. "I do too."

It would be nice to have a familiar face along since I was definitely stepping out of my comfort zone. I mean I knew most of the people I was traveling with casually, but we weren't that close.

Rolling a shirt dress so it wouldn't wrinkle in the bag I stopped and looked up at Harper. "You're sure I'm not crazy for going?"

"You'd be crazy not to go. Now stop worrying."

"Okay," I sighed.

The plane left tonight. I had a long drive ahead of me but I'd been too nervous and excited—not to mention busy—to eat. I'd had plenty of coffee though and I was starting to feel jittery.

The only good thing was I hadn't had much time to stress over the Cash situation. I'd firmly put him on the back burner. Something to be dealt with when I returned.

I did wish I had time to check on the calf before I left though. And on top of my worry over the calf, I was concerned about the kid. Was he still sitting in a cell? Would my letter help in court?

So many loose ends. Too many. They were all going to haunt me in Paris. I knew it.

"I have never seen someone look so miserable to be going on a fabulous trip." Harper shook her head.

I sighed. "I'm just nervous about getting to the airport in time. And I didn't sleep great with all the excitement. I'm hungry too. I really didn't eat today."

Harper's eyes widened. "Then eat something."

"I guess I should run out and grab something for lunch. You wanna come?" I asked.

She glanced at her cell phone. "Actually, I've got a call with my editor in a little while so I'd better get home. But you call me if you need anything else. And text from the airport so I know you made it all right."

"I will." I nodded, wishing again she'd be riding shot gun in my truck for that three plus hour drive.

I shoved the rest of my pile of things I'd be bringing into the bag and zipped it up.

Everything I needed was packed and ready to go.

I'd taken care of everything, except for myself. I really did need to get some food in my stomach so I walked down Main Street. I figured I could pick up a sandwich at the deli counter at the gas station.

Not gourmet fare but they had good cold cuts and fresh rolls and the prices were decent. And I could eat half now and save the other half for the drive. Besides, I liked to shop local whenever possible and while the diner remained closed, food pickings were slim on Main Street in Mudville.

The best part with getting the sandwich was that I could cross the street from the gas station and pick up something sweet at Bethany's.

Happy with my plan, it wasn't too long before I had a brown bag with my roast beef and horseradish cheese with mayo and lettuce on a roll in one hand and was pushing through the door into the bakery.

But instead of the view I'd been expecting— Bethany behind a glass case filled with tasty confections—I was greeted by a very different scene.

I'd recognize the ass in those jeans anywhere. Just as I recognized the man facing away from me and leaning on the counter.

Bethany's head popped into view as she leaned to one side to see around Cash. "Red. Hi. I thought you might have left already."

Cash turned to see me now too. "Hi."

"Uh, hi." I dragged my gaze off him and to Bethany. "I'm leaving in like an hour. I just needed some sustenance."

"Let me pack you a box of treats for the road." Bethany was off in back before I could even thank her. That left me alone in front with Cash.

"You're going somewhere?" he asked.

In this town, the only surprise was that he hadn't already heard.

I nodded. "Yeah. Paris, actually."

I laughed at how that still sounded ridiculous when I said it, and I'd had two days to get used to the idea.

His eyes popped wide. "Paris?"

"Yup. Can you believe it? When I get calls from men it's usually a scammer. But this one here gets invites to Paris," Bethany joked, back with a white box in her hand that she proceeded to fill with things from in the case.

I saw Cash react to her statement.

"He's from the resellers organization I belong to. It's their trip." I didn't know why I felt I had to explain to Cash, but I did, even if he had been looking awfully cozy with Bethany when I'd walked in.

He wouldn't do that, would he? Flirt with my best friend? Yes, actually he might. He was a big flirt usually. With me. With everyone in town. Even some of the old biddies would blush when Cash paid them attention. But would he do more than that? It wouldn't go any further with Bethany. Right? The voice in the back of my mind nagged with the reminder that he'd certainly done more with me.

"I need to get going but I'll talk to you later," Cash said, interrupting my thoughts.

"Yup." Bethany nodded, and I realized he'd been speaking to her, making plans to talk later.

Just *talk?* Talk about what?

My mind raced with more crazy thoughts as he turned to where I stood between him and the door. I might be silly, and jealous, and ridiculous because I was sure there was nothing going on, but I had to put all that away now because I needed to know about the calf.

"Is every*thing* and everybody at the farm all right?" I asked, hoping he got the meaning of my loaded question about the contraband cow hiding out at his place.

A small smile tipped up the corner of his mouth. "Yes. Every*thing* and everybody at the farm are just fine."

"Good. Good." I nodded, feeling relieved.

The smile faded as he said, "Have a good trip, Red."

That might have been the most formal goodbye Cashel Morgan had ever given me. And I had to wonder, why?

CHAPTER TWENTY-THREE

Cash

I walked into the sheriff's department later that afternoon and of course Carson was behind the desk.

How the hell long was his shift anyway? I'd been hoping that since we couldn't get here until Bethany's afternoon help had arrived, I might have a hope of not seeing this man. No such luck.

Although the other deputy, John Callahan, was such a dick I guess I should count myself lucky. I probably had a much better chance of accomplishing what I'd come here to do with Carson behind the desk—even if the man was after my girl.

I smothered a snort. *My girl.* Yeah right.

Red was on her way to Paris with another guy. That fact made Carson look like a lot less of a threat than he had before.

"Hey, Carson."

"Cash." He nodded then his attention moved to Bethany, a couple of feet behind me.

She took a step forward with the offering we had both

thought would be a good idea. A box full of pastries from her bakery. "Hey Carson. I brought these over for you guys."

He lifted the lid on the box she'd set on his desk. "Thanks. Appreciate it."

His gaze cut back to me. He was clearly wondering what the purpose of this visit was. I guess I couldn't blame him.

"Is the kid still here?" I asked.

"Yup. Still here."

Jeez. Two nights in a cell, at that age. That sucked. Poor kid. It made it even more important that I see him, if only to ease his mind that the pup was okay.

"You get anything more on him? A name? A hit on a missing child's report?"

He shook his head. "Nope."

I didn't know if it was that we'd been teammates back at Mudville High, or that I'd been the one to finally catch the kid that made Carson give me answers. I was just happy to get them.

The kid was a tough one. I had to give him that. Holding strong and not answering anything. Either that or he was so afraid of going back to wherever he'd run from, a holding cell in Mudville was preferable. That wasn't a comforting thought.

"I was hoping we could talk to him."

"Both of you want to see him?" Carson's gaze cut between us.

Bethany nodded. "Yes, please. If possible."

He folded his arms, brows drawn low. He was waiting for an explanation. I could tell, even if he hadn't outright asked for one.

I decided to give him one. The truth. "I was hoping we could get something out of him. Some info."

"Why would he talk to you two when he won't talk to me?" Carson asked.

I lifted a brow, glancing at his uniform.

"Besides the fact that I'm a deputy?" Carson continued, answering his own question.

I thought that was reason enough. But of course, we had another reason too. If the boy was a runaway foster kid, I thought maybe Bethany could bond with him. But that wasn't my story to tell.

Even though Boone had known about Bethany's past, I didn't know how many other people in town knew that about her. Or if she wanted it kept quiet.

I glanced at her, looking for answers.

She met my gaze and then turned to Carson. "From what Cash told me, there's a chance the boy ran away from an undesirable situation. Possibly a foster home."

"If that's true, then why are there no reports?" Carson asked.

"Because sometimes the foster family won't report it. For a number of reasons," she explained. "They don't want the black mark on their record. They're hoping the child will come back. They're hoping to get away with no one discovering he's missing until the next home inspection so they'll continue to get paid for him."

Carson's eyes narrowed. "You know a lot about this."

She nodded. "I do."

"You work for child welfare before you started baking?" he asked.

"No." She shook her head.

Carson's expression softened before his gaze cut to me.

227

My bet was he'd guessed where Bethany's experience came from.

He didn't push Bethany to reveal what he no doubt suspected was the truth about her past. He just grabbed the keys and turned toward the back. "Follow me back to the interrogation room."

Crap. I hated that Carson was acting like a good guy. I was going to have to start to like him again.

My gaze cut to Bethany. She flashed me a thumbs up. I nodded and followed Carson back to the now familiar room.

So far so good. Now if only the kid would tell us what was going on in his life so maybe I could help him. Bethany and I had had a nice talk, before Red walked in and dropped that damn Paris bombshell on me, blowing my concentration all to hell.

But before that I had begun to make a plan. What if I took the kid in? Or rather Morgan Farm did. As a single man, they might not allow me to do it alone. But if we took him in as a family, it might work.

He'd have a good home. A mother and father and three older brothers. There was a small room in the back of the house that we used kind of like an office. At least that's where we kept the printer and the big old desktop computer.

We could put a bed in there for him. It wasn't too far from the pantry where Boone was setting up the puppy to be house trained. He could go to Mudville High during the day. And help out with some of the chores afternoons and on weekends to earn some spending money.

I liked the idea. Boone loved it. He liked kids—maybe because sometimes he acted like one himself. Hell, even Stone didn't have anything bad to say about it. That was a miracle.

But most important was that my parents had agreed, which was pretty amazing considering I sprung it on them right after I presented them with the new puppy they hadn't asked for.

They'd sat and listened to what I had to say. What I knew about the kid, which wasn't as much as I'd like. What he'd done, which wasn't exactly good, but was understandable given the circumstances. And they'd agreed. If he needed a home, we had one to give.

Once Bethany had offered to help guide us through the process, the one big thing left to do was talk to the kid. Find out what his situation really was and see if we should bother starting the official paperwork with child services.

Of course, getting the boy to talk to me was another issue.

I saw the kid's shock when he came in and saw me sitting there. He glanced at Bethany and then back to me as he sat, silent. Watching. Waiting.

Carson must have gotten the sense, just like I did, that the kid wasn't going to talk as long as there was an officer of the law in the room.

He cut his gaze to me and said, "Knock when you're ready." Then he was gone and I could get to my plan.

I took my cell out and swiped through until I found the picture I wanted. I turned it to him. He visibly let out a breath of relief at the photo of Romeo sound asleep in our old dog bed, his two front legs wrapped around his new chew toy.

"He's all right?"

"Yup. Happy. Healthy. I don't know what you named him, but we're calling him Romeo at my house. Because he likes to kiss us so much."

Amazingly, a small smile tipped up the corner of the

kid's mouth.

"So, what should I call you?" I asked. It was a shot in the dark, but who knows? It might work.

The kid's gaze cut to Bethany and I guessed what he was thinking. I might have earned a small amount of trust from him because of the dog. But she hadn't. He must think she was with child services and didn't want to answer with her in the room.

"This is my friend, Bethany. She owns the bakery on Main Street. And actually, she's good friends with Red, from the resale shop. Bethany brought over some pastries for the deputy. Kind of a bribe so he'd let us visit with you." I continued to talk since he wasn't. "I'm glad he did let us see you. I wanted to show you that picture of Romeo, so you didn't worry about him. Maybe Deputy Bekker will let you have one of the honey buns Bethany brought. They're the best ones in town."

"They're the only ones in town but thank you." Bethany smiled. "And it's very nice to meet you. I got to spend some time with Romeo last night at Cash's house. He's a sweetie."

Bethany and I chatted away to the kid, even if he was silently stoic in his lack of responses.

She glanced sideways at me and then leaned forward to focus directly on the kid.

"It's none of my business. Your situation. Your life. Even what your name is. But I wanted you to know something about me. I grew up in foster care. From the time I was ten, after I lost my mom. Never knew my dad." She swallowed hard. "Anyway. I know what it's like to have a tough childhood. To want to run away. To actually do it. If you need to talk, I'll listen. And if not, I understand that too."

"Bart."

"Excuse me," I asked, when the kid's comment surprised and confused me.

"My name. Bart."

Bethany smiled and asked, "Your mother a Simpsons fan by chance?"

"Yeah." He nodded. After a few moments of silence, he said, "She got cancer."

She pressed her lips together. "I'm very sorry, Bart."

"Me too," I agreed, doing my best to keep my cool and not spook the kid now that he was finally talking.

There were a dozen things I wanted to ask him but was afraid to. I could only hope Bethany and I were on the same page and she'd ask them for me.

"Who were you living with? After?" she asked.

"My grandma at first. Then . . . she died too."

Jesus. This poor kid.

"Where did you go then?" Bethany asked gently.

"Foster family."

"Why did you leave?" She was asking the hard questions now and I held my breath to see how he would respond.

"They weren't nice." Three simple words, but they held the weight of so many more.

Bethany swallowed audibly before she nodded. "Yeah. I lived with a couple of families who weren't very nice either. Then, I got lucky. I got adopted by the nicest family ever."

Now that the conversation was starting to flow, I decided to satisfy my own curiosity.

"How long were you on your own, Bart?"

"About a month."

"How did you survive that long?" Bethany asked.

He shrugged. "People ignore a kid. They forget I'm there and talk. I could see the warehouse was empty but it was cold in there. When I overheard about that big house on Second Street being empty, I moved there." He lifted his shoulder again.

I had to hand it to him. He was resourceful. But the fact he'd kept himself and that puppy from freezing or starving was enough to have both of us shocked into silence.

Finally, he asked, "Are they going to send me back?"

"I honestly don't know," she answered.

I wanted to tell him my plan, give him hope that the same could happen to him like it had for Bethany. He could find a great family too. My family.

But it was too early. I had no clue if I could make it happen and getting his hopes up for nothing would be cruel.

Hell, I didn't know what would happen. Once social services figured out where he'd run from, would they just send him back there, no matter how bad Bart claimed the family was?

I didn't know the system. I'm not sure even Bethany did after being out of it for so many years.

Bart focused on me. "You'll keep him? Romeo."

"Yes. He's got a good home with my family on our farm for the rest of his life. He's going to learn to help with the herd. He'll have lots of friends. Animals and people. I promise."

The kid nodded.

He seemed more concerned about the puppy than

himself. Maybe that was because he realized he had no control over his own life, but by trusting me, he'd at least made sure the dog would be all right.

I saw Bethany biting her lip and looking close to tears. Time to get her out of here.

The kid's big brown eyes followed my movement as I stood. "We're going to go. But I'll try to see you again real soon. Okay?"

He lifted one shoulder, like it didn't matter. He was trying to play it cool. Act the tough guy who didn't care. I knew because it was what I would have done in his position.

Bethany stood and walked around the table. She leaned down and hugged the boy. Then, without saying a word, she moved to the door and knocked to get Carson's attention.

I asked Carson if he could sneak the kid a honey bun before I thanked him and followed Bethany outside where she stood waiting for me.

"Thanks for coming with me."

She nodded. "Of course. Anything I can do to help, I'm happy to do." The words were polite but her voice shook as she delivered them.

This had affected her. I could only guess Bart's situation brought back too many memories of her own past. Coming from a Norman Rockwell family like I did, how could I relate to what she was feeling?

I couldn't, so I did the best thing I could at the moment. I wrapped my arm around her shoulder and squeezed, then said, "You wanna stop for a drink? On me."

She laughed. "Yeah. Actually. That'd be good."

"And maybe while we're there you can tell me how the

fuck Red came to be in Paris with some guy," I suggested.

She lifted a brow and glanced at me, a sly smirk on her lips. "That bother you? Her being in Paris with some guy?"

"No. I mean, I'm just concerned. What do we know about this guy? Was this thing planned? I didn't hear a word about it until she was leaving. And did you see her Instagram? It looks like she went right from the airport to some fancy cocktail party."

By the time I finished my rant, Bethany was covering her mouth to hide her laughter.

I frowned. "What's so funny?"

"You, Cashel Morgan. In fact, all of you Morgan boys. It took Stone months to get off his ass and tell Harper how he really felt about her. How long is it going to take you?"

"I don't understand what you're talking about." I scowled.

"No, I guess you wouldn't. Must be a family gene." Shaking her head, she reached for the truck's handle.

On the other side of the vehicle I stood, keys in my hand, not moving as my mind spun with the comparison. Harper and Stone were in love. Their situation was nothing like the one with me and Red.

Was it?

Crap.

She peered over the hood at me. "We going?"

The question knocked me out of my stupor but not out of my misery. "Yeah."

I could certainly use a beer about now.

And when we got to the bar and I made the mistake of pulling out my cell and looking at Red's Instagram while Bethany went to the ladies' room, I knew I needed more

234

than just a beer. Because there she stood, hugged up on Mr. Paris, a glass of champagne in her hand and the widest smile I'd ever seen on her face.

Fuck.

"What can I get ya?" Lainey asked me.

I tossed my cell onto the bar, angry at the device and pretty much everything else in the world right now, including myself.

"Shot of bourbon, Lainey. Make that a double."

Bethany was just gonna have to drive my truck, because the way I was feeling, one drink wasn't going to be enough.

CHAPTER TWENTY-FOUR

Red

"You make it home yet?" Frank asked me over the cell phone.

"Just pulled into the driveway and walked into my place."

"Good."

"Where are you?" I asked, turning on the heater since it was freezing after my not being home for a week.

"About to board my flight."

I cringed. "Sorry. I feel bad."

"Because you're home and I'm not? You should." He laughed and then said, "Just kidding. I was actually happy to have a few hours layover between the two long flights. I got a decent meal. Stretched my legs. It's all good. Of course, it would have been more fun if I'd had company. But no, *you* wanted to get on the road right away instead of hanging out in JFK with me. I don't know what you were thinking."

I heard the humor in his tone and smiled. "Yeah. I'm selfish that way."

"Anyway, I'm glad you decided to come on the trip, Red."

"Me too. And thank you. It wouldn't have happened without you."

"Yeah, well, I'm a good guy that way," he joked. "Now, when you decide you've had enough of redneck resale in frigid upstate New York and finally move out to Cali where the sun always shines, I'll take you to even more fabulous places. Of course, that's only if you don't end up married to that farmer first."

"Frank! I told you about him in confidence." I plopped down on the sofa and covered my face with one hand, embarrassed by my heated cheeks even though he couldn't see me.

"No. You told me that because you drank half a bottle of champagne on an empty stomach. I don't recall any confidentiality agreement." Frank chuckled.

I remembered drinking and talking much too much and regretting it in the morning—and not just from the hangover. "Ugh. I'm hanging up now."

"Your hanging up won't make me magically forget all you told me about your farm boy Cashel—that was his name, right?"

"Yes." I groaned.

"But you're off the hook anyway because they're starting to board my flight, so I'll let you go. I'm sure you want to unpack that pretty new dress you bought and see how Cashel likes it."

I shook my head at myself and my own foolishness. "Goodbye, Frank. Safe flight."

"Goodbye, Red. Talk to you soon."

I disconnected and groaned again when I remembered how much money I'd spent on that new dress, all because I'd been swept up in the magic of Paris. I'd also had a bit of wine in me.

And yes, maybe I splurged on the dress because of Cash. He had been on my mind way too much on that trip. Which was ridiculous.

We weren't dating. We were friends. Friends who made the mistake of accidentally having sex. That was all.

So why did I want to see him so badly now that I was home?

I had to resist the impulse. I'd look like a loser if the first thing I did when I walked in the door was text Cash. It would seem like a booty call and I'd look pitiful.

Huffing out a breath, I stalked to the fridge, and realized that I had even less to eat in the house than usual. No milk. No eggs. Maybe there was a freezer burned frozen pizza if I was lucky.

After eating French cuisine for a week, I was ready for some good old American food—and American-sized portions since the French ate like birds. I swear I'd never seen so little food on a plate in my life, even as an appetizer, and in Paris they'd call that a meal.

I wasn't in the mood for a cold sandwich, and though I'd love to indulge in something from Bethany's after dinner, I wanted a good hot meal first.

There were slim pickings in Mudville for good hot food as long as the diner and the historic Mudd House remained for sale and were closed for business.

It would have to be the Muddy River Inn for me, for wings or maybe a burger. Oh, and definitely an order of hot hand-cut French fries—which were *not* French, by the way. I'd asked while I was there and had gotten laughed at.

The drive from the airport in Queens had been long. The flight on the private jet from Paris to JFK even longer. I was ready to take a hot shower and put on some warm comfy flannel PJs.

Maybe I'd call in an order and pick up my meal to go. It would feel good to be home after being away.

I made the call, opting for Garlic Parmesan Boneless Chicken Wings and fries, and adding on an order of fried pickles too at the last minute. When Lainey told me it would be twenty minutes before my order was ready, I took the time to wash my face and brush my teeth.

I'd been traveling for what felt like days. It had been too long since I'd felt clean.

I didn't bother changing. I'd do that later after a shower when I could slide right into pajamas. Happy with that plan, I pulled my jacket and gloves back on and got back into the truck. At least this trip was only a few miles rather than a few hours.

"Red, how was your trip?" Lainey, the bar owner and sometimes the cook, bartender and waitress depending on staff that day, smiled as I walked in the door.

"Great. Really amazing."

"It looked like it from the pictures I saw."

I frowned. The only pictures from the trip were on my Instagram.

"You stalking my Instagram?" I joked, impressed since I hadn't thought Lainey, who was probably close to my grandmother's age, was on social media.

She dismissed that with a wave of her hand. "I couldn't be bothered with that stuff. But Bethany and Cashel were in here and showed me some of the pictures you put online. Hang on and let me grab your food. Carter's just bagging it up."

My stomach twisted as the last thing I wanted was the food. Bethany and Cashel were at the bar together. What did that mean? *Was* there something going on with him and Bethany?

I couldn't blame her if there was. I'd kept my thing with Cash—whatever it was—secret from her.

In hindsight that had been epically dumb. It could cost me my best friend, because how in the world could I continue to be around Bethany if she ended up dating—or worse married to—the man I was falling for?

I somehow managed to pay for my food and keep up my half of the conversation with Lainey until I got out to my truck. But once there, I was close to losing it.

The food in the bag on the passenger seat filled the truck with what should have been an enticing aroma. I should go directly home and eat it while it was still hot. Instead I found myself pulling along the curb in front of Bethany's shop.

I was a glutton for punishment, but I needed to know if they were together. What I'd do with that knowledge once I had it, I didn't know.

As a red head, I'd never been able to hide my emotions. Angry—my face turned red. Embarrassed—my cheeks turned pink.

I couldn't name all the emotions I felt right now— sad and upset were right up there at the top of the list—but I'd have to try to hide it all.

Inside, Bethany was behind the counter. "Hey. Oh my God, you're home. I wasn't sure what time you'd be getting back."

"I just got back." I was grateful she was here working and not out on a date with Cash or something. "So, what did I miss while I was gone?"

She laughed. "This is Mudville. Not a whole lot going on here. But you—you were in Paris. How was it?"

"Amazing," I said, though I was less enthused about the trip now that I knew Cash and Bethany had been going out in my absence.

"Yeah? That's so great. I hope you took more pictures than those few you put on Instagram."

The knife in my heart felt real as I remembered Lainey's comment about Bethany and Cash checking out my Instagram at the bar.

How could he do that? Sleep with me. Then go on

a date with my best friend, and while on that date look at my Instagram?

"You all right?" Bethany asked. "You look kind of out of it."

"I'm just tired. Long flight. Long drive. Jet lag." All of the above applied, but I would have navigated it like a champ if my heart wasn't broken in two. "I'll be fine once I get some sleep."

If I could sleep in my misery.

Bethany nodded. "You probably should go home and go to bed. It's like the middle of the night over there, right?"

"Yeah, it's pretty late." I'd been calculating the time difference the whole time I'd been away so I could imagine where Cash might be, what he might be doing. But I never imagined what he was doing could be my best friend.

"Well, before you go, I have to tell you one thing." She leaned forward conspiratorially. "Cash was crazed when he saw those pictures of you and Frank on your Instagram."

The topic of Cash captured my full attention, but what she said didn't make much sense. "What?"

"Yup." She nodded, smiling. "I think he likes you."

Maybe I was more tired than I realized because none of this made sense. Why was Bethany saying that if she was with Cash?

Because maybe she wasn't with him. For the first time, that actually seemed like an option. But then what were they doing having dinner together? They weren't friends that I knew of.

"How do you know?" I asked.

"I'm working on a—um—project with him so we've been spending some time together and every time I'm with him, he's asking me what's up with you and Frank."

This wasn't helping my confusion.

I needed more information to wipe all suspicion out of my mind—and I really wanted to do that because I didn't want to lose Bethany or Cash.

Even if we were just friends with benefits, life without him in it in some capacity would stink.

"What kind of project are you two working on together?"

She cringed. "You know you're my best friend, right?"

"Yes?" My suspicion came back full force.

"Well, I still can't tell you."

"What?" My eyes widened.

"It's just—he's trying to keep it on the down low right now and it's not even a certainty that it's all going to work out."

I was ready to crawl out of my skin. I hated secrets.

Oh, I liked them when I was in on them and I'd take a secret to my grave when someone confided in me, but being on the outside of one? That I couldn't stand.

Especially when it involved two people close to me.

Bethany must have seen how upset I was. "Go over to the farm. Talk to Cash. He'll probably tell you. No, you know what? I'm sure he'll tell you. It just can't come from me. Okay?" She cringed again, obviously not any happier about this secret than I was.

I blew out a breath, but once I allowed myself to reason things out and stop reacting emotionally, I realized something. Maybe this had to do with the calf. Maybe Bethany was helping Cash with that. How, I couldn't fathom, but if she thought I didn't know, she would keep his secret. It could get him in a lot of trouble if she didn't.

And even if I was totally off base, it was a good excuse to go to the farm and try to find Cash.

I had another reason. I had been away for a week. Of course I'd want to check on the calf after all that time.

For better or worse, I was going to the farm and getting to the bottom of this.

CHAPTER TWENTY-FIVE

Cash

"Always stand on the left side of a horse when you're leading him or if you're getting up into the saddle," I told Bart.

"Why?"

The kid liked to ask questions. All. The. Time.

That was fine. At least it showed he was interested in what I was saying. The problem arose when I didn't have an answer to his many questions.

"Because that's how we train them," I said, knowing if he came back and asked why again, I wouldn't be able to come up with a very good answer. *Because that's how it's done* didn't feel like a good enough reason but it was the only one I had.

There was nothing like an inquisitive child to make a man feel dumb. One of the many things no one ever told me about kids. Or maybe they did and I just wasn't listening at the time.

This could be karma paying me back for all the times I'd given my parents grief.

Well played, karma. Well played.

I paused, waiting for a follow-up from Bart. When none came, I let out a breath in relief and moved on. "So, remember what I told you about holding the lead rope?"

"Never wrap it around my hand."

"Good. And why is that?" I asked.

"Because I don't want to get dragged to death if he takes off running."

I hadn't put it quite in those words . . . "Um. Right. You don't want to get your hand tangled up and not be able to get free."

So far, the kid had shown a natural affinity for working with animals.

He'd taken to the horses right off. He was up early every morning this week to help me with the cows. And of course, he and Romeo were inseparable. Like they were tied together. If the kid stopped short, the pup ran into the back of him.

Boone and Stone were both great with him. Mom and Dad seemed good with the arrangement so far. But there was the definite feeling of a cloud hanging over us as we all waited to see what would happen.

Bart was here as a stop gap measure, to get him out of the sheriff's holding cell until a more permanent solution could be found.

Whether that would be a juvenile detention center or foster care was up to the judge, I supposed. Since we'd applied to take him in, as his new foster family, this time was as much a trial period for us as for him.

But it was going good so far. No one could say otherwise. Of course, since an inspection could come at any time, I was on my best behavior since Bart had moved in. No trips to the bar for me. Not even a beer with dinner. No staying out late. And, most importantly, no one in town could find out about my having Red's controversial calf.

Between tending to the calf, the puppy and the kid, and worrying about toeing the line in the eyes of child services, I was pretty much having no fun of any kind. But with Red in Paris with that guy, I wasn't really in a fun mood anyhow so it didn't much matter.

And hey, who said playing video games every night with the kid couldn't be fun?

"Your girlfriend is here," Bart said, the comb in his hand as he paused in his work on the horse's tangled mane.

I frowned. "What? I don't have a girlfriend—"

I stopped mid-sentence and spun to face the driveway when I realized there was one person who Bart might assume was my girlfriend.

"That's not what I heard. *Oh, Red.*" Bart did his poor imitation of me again, but I couldn't care he was making fun—couldn't be appalled he might actually have heard us in bed—because Red's truck was in the driveway.

She must be back from that damned eternal trip to France. Thank God for that. When I wasn't concerned with the kid, I'd done nothing but think about Red. About us. Together.

Of course, that was all a waste of time if she was

with Mr. Paris. I guess I was about to find that out since she had parked the truck and was about to get out.

The sun was starting to set. It was a good excuse to ditch the kid, just for now. This discussion required privacy. "Hey, kid. Why don't you go inside and get cleaned up and see if my Mom needs you to set the table for dinner or something."

He smirked. "You two wanna be *alone*." He made the last word long and suggestive.

"You'll be alone when I toss you in the hay loft and take away the ladder if you don't stop being a smart ass."

He grinned as he handed me the comb and walked toward the house, Romeo at his heels. I unhooked the cross ties and led the horse into the stall, locking the door as Red made her way over to me.

"Hey," I said when she was close enough to hear.

"Hey." She glanced at the kid on his way toward the house. Her barely-there strawberry blonde brows drew low. "Is that—"

"The kid I tackled in your driveway? Yeah." I glanced from the kid back to Red. "Some stuff's happened while you've been gone."

My only hope was that all the major events that had taken place had been in Mudville and Red didn't have any life altering news from Paris for me.

"Apparently." Her eyes, the lightest shade of blue, focused on mine. "Wanna tell me about it?"

"Yeah. I do." I wanted nothing more than to talk

to Red. And not a casual conversation either.

We were long overdue for a real heart-to-heart.

Time to let her in on the discussions I'd been holding with myself. How I felt about her. And the scary part—how she felt about me. And that damn guy in Paris.

I drew in a breath. "It turns out Bart—that's the kid—is a runaway. Long story short, his mom died, he lived with his grandma until she died, then he got put in a not so great foster home. He ran away. And the damn kid's been surviving on his own, while caring for a puppy, for a month. That's why he broke into your store. To get the sleeping bag to try and keep warm."

"Wow." She shook her head.

"Yeah." I nodded. "He's a tough little kid. He's got a smart mouth on him sometimes, no doubt, but he's quick to learn and a hard worker. And he loves animals. He's real good with them."

"Sounds a little like you." She smiled.

I laughed. "Yeah. I've thought that a time or two myself."

"So you, what? Hired him to work here?" she asked, sounding amazed.

I was grateful she wasn't angry. Afterall, he had stolen from her store. But I should have realized she'd understand why I had to take him in and forgive why he'd done what he'd done.

She had written a letter to the judge and didn't press charges, according to Carson. That had helped the kid as much as us taking him in.

"Yes and no." I wobbled my head in answer to her question about his working for Morgan Farm. "He's getting an allowance for the work he's doing, but it's more than that. We're trying to get him placed here. As his permanent foster home. Navigating the system has been a nightmare. Red tape. Inspections. Waiting for an answer. But Bethany's been helping Mom and Dad as much as she can with the paperwork."

"Bethany." Red's eyes widened as she let out a big breath. "That's why you've been spending so much time with her."

"Well, it hasn't been all that much time . . ." I realized it hadn't been a question. More of a eureka moment for Red as she put two and two together. "Wait. Were you jealous? Of me and Bethany?"

I couldn't control the smile spreading across my face.

"No." Her pout was adorable. "Maybe. A little."

"There's nothing to be jealous of."

"I know that now. I just didn't know what to think. You were in the bakery the day I left. Then I heard you were with her at the bar . . ." She lifted one shoulder.

The Mudville gossip mill was still hard at work. No surprise there. At least this time it was working in my favor. If it took making Red a little bit jealous to get her to admit she had feelings for me, I'd take it.

And since she'd been honest with me, I figured I'd better do the same. "So, while we're on the subject of jealousy—"

"I'm not jealous . . ." She rolled her eyes at me, then added, "At least, not anymore."

I continued in spite of her interruption, "What's up with you and Mr. Paris?"

"Are *you* jealous?" she asked.

"So fucking jealous I could spit," I admitted, taking a step closer.

A smile lit her face, but all I cared about was that she took a step toward me, putting her in touching distance. "Is it bad I'm a little bit happy about that?" she asked.

"The only thing I want is for you to be happy." I reached out to pull her closer. "Well, maybe that's not the *only thing* I want."

I held her close and leaned low toward her mouth.

"I can think of a few other things that will make us both happy," I said.

"So, are we going to continue the way we were? Sneaking around in my apartment?"

"Is that what you want?" I asked.

Yeah, the time I'd spent in her place had been some of the best hours of my life, but I wanted more than that.

"What do you want?" she asked, answering my question with a question.

I wanted her to belong to me and no one else. I wanted the right to punch Carson and Mr. Paris in the face if they even looked at her. I wanted to fall asleep with her in my arms and wake up to her smiling face in the morning.

And I really wanted to make love to her all night, every night. Possibly for the rest of my life.

That all seemed a bit much to ask of her at this stage in our relationship, so I started small. "I want you to be my girl."

She bit her lip. "Publicly?"

I frowned. "Of course, publicly. What do you think? I'm going to hide you in the shed with the calf?" I asked.

She shook her head and smiled. "That's what I want too. To be your girl."

"Good." I tried to hide how choked up I was feeling by pulling her tight against me and pressing her cheek against my chest. I kissed the top of her head, then rested my head on top of hers. "So now that we're official, you can come inside with me and explain to Mom and Dad why there's a stolen calf in our shed. I haven't gotten around to telling them yet."

She pulled back and glared at me. "She's not stolen."

"Tell that to that bastard at the auction house. Nope, that little girly is most definitely red hot goods." I grinned. "Just like her mamma."

When she opened her mouth to fight me some more, I decided to end the debate the most pleasant way I knew how. I leaned down and captured her lips with mine.

She melted against me and stopped fighting, which was exactly as I'd hoped.

The kiss got heated fast. I'd been a week without

the woman I was falling in love with.

She wrapped her arms around my waist and pressed close and I started to wish we were anywhere but here.

Leaning back, I said, "Wanna go visit your calf quick?"

She got a sly smile on her face as she pressed her lower half tighter against the very obvious hard-on in my jeans. "You asking me to sneak away with you to the shed?"

I grinned. There was no hiding what I was thinking from her. "I am."

"All right," she agreed, and I knew, that calf wasn't going to be the only red hot thing in that shed.

EPILOGUE

Red

It was hot, which was odd since it wasn't even May first yet and this was Mudville, New York, capitol of cold rainy spring weather and, of course, the accompanying mud.

Though Cash was probably happy about the warm weather. It could help the corn grow. I was still new at the ins and outs of farming. Bart though had taken to farming like he'd been born into it.

I saw him out there in the field now, bouncing along in the seat of the tractor as Boone rode along with him. Proof that all it took was a good family to bring out the best in the kid.

Without Cash, things could have turned out so differently for Bart. I hated to even think about what might have become of him.

Turning away from the field, I walked around my truck and toward the farm stand. I knew Cash said they were getting it ready to open for the season.

Besides annual routine maintenance, they'd be

building some more display shelves inside. I'd talked them into carrying some goods from local artisans. With their built-in traffic, it only made sense to sell complementary items that their customer base would be interested in.

In addition to their usual fresh fruit and vegetables, meat and dairy, they'd expand to carrying other stuff. Jams and jellies. Local honey. Bees wax products like candles, hand salve and lip balm. Homemade soap. Fresh flowers. Painted signs. Wood and metal crafts. Even canvas shopping bags with the Morgan Farm Market logo on the front—the logo which now featured a picture of my truck because when Cash asked, I couldn't say no.

I pretty much couldn't say no to Cash about anything. The man was persuasive in so many ways, there was nothing I'd deny him. So far, that had been working out pretty well, for both of us.

There was a car parked right up in front of the door of the stand, which was odd since they weren't open for business for the season yet.

Apparently, someone had been driving by and saw the Morgan truck parked there and thought they were open.

When I got up to the doorway, I stopped dead, because the person I saw was the last one I wanted to see.

A memory hit me of the last time I'd seen Betty Frank.

It had been that day in my store—that most horrible and wonderful day.

The day half of the town of Mudville had turned against me because I'd dare to take in the runaway calf. Betty had come into the shop to accuse me of letting the calf loose and setting up the reward to get publicity for my shop.

I'd been close to losing it. That's when Cash had pulled me outside to the carriage house—where I had lost it. And where he'd comforted me. Oh, how he'd comforted me.

It was a day I'd never forget. And here she was, bringing back all those memories. Both the good and the bad.

"I'm sorry. No." Inside, Cash shook his head.

I could see him clearly through the doorway. His stance broadcast his feelings more than his words. His feet were set wide, his arms crossed over his chest, and the steady shake of his head left no question. Whatever Betty had asked for, he wasn't giving it to her.

I pulled back a few inches so I'd be less visible as I spied, more than curious. And, I had to admit, feeling pretty satisfied the horrible woman wasn't going to get her way.

"But you always give me corn for my chicken. I come here and your brother gives me a big sack of dried corn."

Ah, yes. Her emotional support chicken.

The one she sometimes brought into the store with her, claiming it was officially registered as a support animal so she was allowed. Granted, no one had ever seen the paperwork, but I had given in and let her bring it inside. It was easier than fighting about it.

I wasn't inclined to do so any more however. *If* she ever came in again after that last encounter.

"Well, my brother's not here," he said, still shaking his head.

"But—"

"Look, they sell fifty-pound bags of cracked corn at the feed store for ten bucks. I suggest you go there."

"But I always got it here for free," she protested.

"Not anymore, you don't," he said.

"Your parents are going to hear about this!"

He laughed. "Go for it. Now if you'll excuse me, I have work to do to prepare for actual paying customers."

With a humph, she spun and I had to jump backwards to not look as if I'd been hovering, eavesdropping.

When she cleared the doorway, she sent me a glare. "You and your boyfriend deserve each other."

I forced a smile. "Thank you. I agree."

She humphed again and stalked to her car. I didn't take the time to watch her leave, though I probably should have, if only to make sure she didn't sideswipe my truck on her way out.

Instead I strode into the building and right up to Cash. I grabbed his face in both hands, stood on tiptoe and pressed a big kiss to his lips. He kissed me back with as much passion as our first kiss. As I hoped he always would.

When I finally pulled away, he said, "What was that for?"

"Just for being you. God, I love you. And I love how you told off Betty Frank."

"I love you too. But ugh, that woman." He shook his head. "I'm shaking, she makes me so mad. How she treated you—"

"It's okay. You were perfect. You *are* perfect."

He blew out a laugh. "I'm not sure even I agree with you on that."

"Nope. You are. Perfect for me."

Cash tipped his head. "All right. I agree to that. We're perfect for each other."

We really were. Even horrible Betty agreed.

"Oh, my God, you guys!" Bethany's voice had me turning, just as I'd been about to kiss my man one more time.

"What's wrong?" I asked.

"You won't believe this," she began.

Cash lifted a brow. "Try us."

"Bart came into the shop after school yesterday to get a cookie."

Cash narrowed his eyes. "He's supposed to come right home after school."

Bethany frowned. "You hush up, Cashel. He deserves a sweet before he starts an afternoon full of chores and homework."

"Yeah," I agreed with Bethany, while shooting Cash a grin.

"Yes, ma'am." He scowled but wrapped an arm around me.

"Anyway, I usually give it to him for free." She pointed a finger at Cash. "Not one word. He always offers to pay but I won't let him."

Cash drew in a breath and let it out in a sigh but kept quiet.

Bethany continued, "So, he brought me a little bundle of letters tied with a ribbon. He said he wanted me to have it as a gift since I'm so nice to him. I thanked him but I was busy. A couple of customers came in so I shoved them under the register and forgot about them until today when I finally took the time to open them up."

"What were they?" I asked, dying to know what had her so excited.

"Rose's old love letters," she burst out.

"What?" I asked, eyes wide.

"Yes! Dated from like World War I."

"Holy cow."

"I bet he found them in the attic of her old house while he was living there," Cash suggested.

My eyes widened with realization. "I bet you're right. Harper and I found an old wedding dress in that attic from about the same era."

"I knew that old bird wasn't done with this town yet." Bethany shook her head. "Those journals in Agnes's attic were just the beginning."

"You're right. We have to tell Harper. She's going to flip." Our resident author would probably get a new book out of them.

"Do you think I should give them to her? Or do you want them?" Bethany asked, sounding a bit less excited at the prospect of parting with the letters.

I realized something. Harper had Stone. I had Cash. But all Bethany had was a job that kept her busy all the time and two best friends who were now so occupied with our boyfriends we weren't there for her as much as we used to be.

Bethany needed these letters. Needed the mystery and the romance in them, more than Harper or me.

"I think you should keep them," I said.

"Really?" she asked.

"Yup. Harper has the journals. I bought half of her possessions from the attic in her old house. I think you should keep the letters. That way we all have a little something from Rose."

"Okay." She nodded, looking happy. "But I'll make sure to scan them like Harper did the journals so we have a digital copy. And I'll take notes and let you guys know what's in them."

Cash let out a snort. "Knowing Rose, God only knows what you're going to find in there."

"I personally can't wait to see." I grinned.

Bethany let out a breath. "Okay. I gotta get back to the bakery. I just couldn't wait to tell you. Talk later?"

"Definitely." I nodded

When she'd gone, Cash smiled at me. "That was

263

nice of you, telling her to keep them. I know you were dying to get your hands on those letters."

I turned to face him. "I'm dying to get my hands on something all right, but it's not those letters."

"Oh, really?" He grinned as I yanked on his belt buckle to pull him closer.

"Can we lock that door for a little while?" I asked, shooting a glance behind me.

"I most definitely can. Or we can leave it open and take our chances." He waggled his eyebrows.

"You are such a bad boy," I reprimanded.

He cocked up a brow. "Obviously you like me bad, so don't expect me to change any time soon."

"I wouldn't want you to."

Our impending kiss was again interrupted, this time by Boone skidding in through the door. "Did you hear?"

"Hear what?" Cash asked sounding less than patient. I knew what he was thinking. He should have locked the door.

Bethany came back inside on Boone's heels and said, "Somebody bought the old diner. Boone just told me outside."

"It's sat empty for eight years. Where did you hear this?" I asked, wide eyed.

"Lainey at the bar," Boone answered. "Some really rich dude from Philly."

Lainey. She was the one person in this town we might actually be able to trust to have accurate information and not just hearsay.

While we all digested that information, Alice Mudd hustled in the door with Mary Brimley hot on her heels.

Next to me, Cash sighed.

I felt his pain. This happened at my store too. If I made the mistake of leaving the door unlocked while I closed up, even if I had turned off the lights and flipped the sign to *Closed*, people still came inside. It never failed.

I squeezed his hand in sympathy as the two old women pushed their way past Boone and Bethany.

"Did you hear ?" Mary asked. She looked and sounded as if she were bursting with information.

I knew what she was going to say. We all did. Though what version we got in this game of small-town telephone from the two old biddies about the sale of the diner should be interesting.

Cash's gaze met mine and again I knew what he was thinking. What we were both thinking. That was the thing about Mudville—the more things changed, the more they stayed the same.

Considering my relationship with Cash was all part of that cycle, I wasn't going to complain. Not one little bit.

I got to be in love with my best friend, and trust me, we were both really enjoying the benefits.

Tonight, my Mudville girl gang and I were going to unearth all of this town's secrets. I couldn't wait.

Dear Reader,

Don't miss Honey Buns for more small town Mudville crazy! There's the appearance of the mysterious millionaire from Philly, more secrets from Rose's letters, and Bethany's love story, all as the reopening of the Mudville Diner turns Main Street on its ear!

Happy Reading!

XOXO
Cat Johnson

ABOUT THE AUTHOR

A top 10 *New York Times* and *USA Today* bestselling author, Cat Johnson writes contemporary romance featuring sexy alpha heroes who often wear cowboy or combat boots. Known for her creative marketing, Cat has sponsored bull-riding cowboys, used bologna to promote her romance novels, and owns a collection of camouflage and cowboy boots for book signings.

She lives in a Queen Anne Victorian on Main Street in a small town in upstate New York with too many cats and chickens, but no pig. Yet.

For more visit CatJohnson.net

Join the mailing list at catjohnson.net/news

Manufactured by Amazon.ca
Bolton, ON

25366026R00159